GWELF: The Survival Guide

GWELF COUNCIL for TOURISM and TRADE

Gwelf: The Survival Guide

Published by Eye of Newt Books Inc. • www.eyeofnewtpress.com
Eye of Newt Books Inc. 56 Edith Drive, Toronto, Ontario, M4R 1C3

Design and layout copyright © 2021, 2022, 2023 Eye of Newt Books Inc.

Text copyright © 2021 Larry MacDougall

Illustrations by Larry MacDougall copyright © 2021 Eye of Newt Books Inc.

CIP data for this book is available from Library and Archives Canada.

ISBN: 978-1-7770817-3-7

10 9 8 7 6 5 4 3

Printed in China

Gwelf

The
SURVIVAL GUIDE

by
LARRY MACDOUGALL

For Patricia

who has been with me every step of the way

TABLE of CONTENTS

Foreword

THE MEMBERS OF THE GWELF COUNCIL FOR Tourism and Trade proudly present the first guide to Gwelf ever formally published and distributed to the Southlands. We have taken it upon ourselves to create what we call a "Survival Guide" in the hopes that it will encourage both tourists and adventurers to come experience and explore our wondrous realm and learn what we have known for years: that Gwelf is an awe-inspiring land steeped in magic and beauty.

Survival is, of course, the critical term. The Region of Gwelf is little known in the Southlands, and what is known is tainted by rumour and half-truth. Often described as haunted and perilous, we want to assure tourist and adventurer alike that the Sparrows and other citizens of the territory have worked hard to create a haven of the riverbank and capital City of Gwelf. It is a place thrumming with activity and rich in culture, a ready location for vacation or launching point for voyage.

The town has grown, as with many urban centres, out of necessity and not strategy. Our lovely Gwelf is unrefined in that it has grown organically over the decades since the rift between Sparrowkind and Ravenkind, owing much of its aesthetic and construction to the landscape on which it was built and to the ingenuity and craftsmanship of the Badger inhabitants here.

Artists, voyeurs, and free spirits are welcome additions to Gwelf, filling our pubs with new faces and stories over homebrewed elderflower ale or becoming tea aficionados at the Rose and Nettle. Adventurers are our most cherished visitors. The treasures and tales brought back by adventurers are added to the memory banks of Gwelf citizens and inured into Gwelf's Archives and history. It is to adventurers that we most highly recommend this guide, whether they seek the thrill of crossing the Albion Bridge, spiritual connection in the Graveyard on Cluster Hill, or high adventure in or beyond the Boreal Mountains, return might be more likely.

We, the Council, are like you, migrants from the Southlands who have turned immigrant through a love for this land. We invite you to join us in this world of opportunity. Whatever it is you dream of in life, you can find it here, as a tourist, entrepreneur, or resident. The road north to Gwelf is long and an adventure in itself, but we are certain that this journey is only the beginning.

Best of luck,

The Council of Gwelf

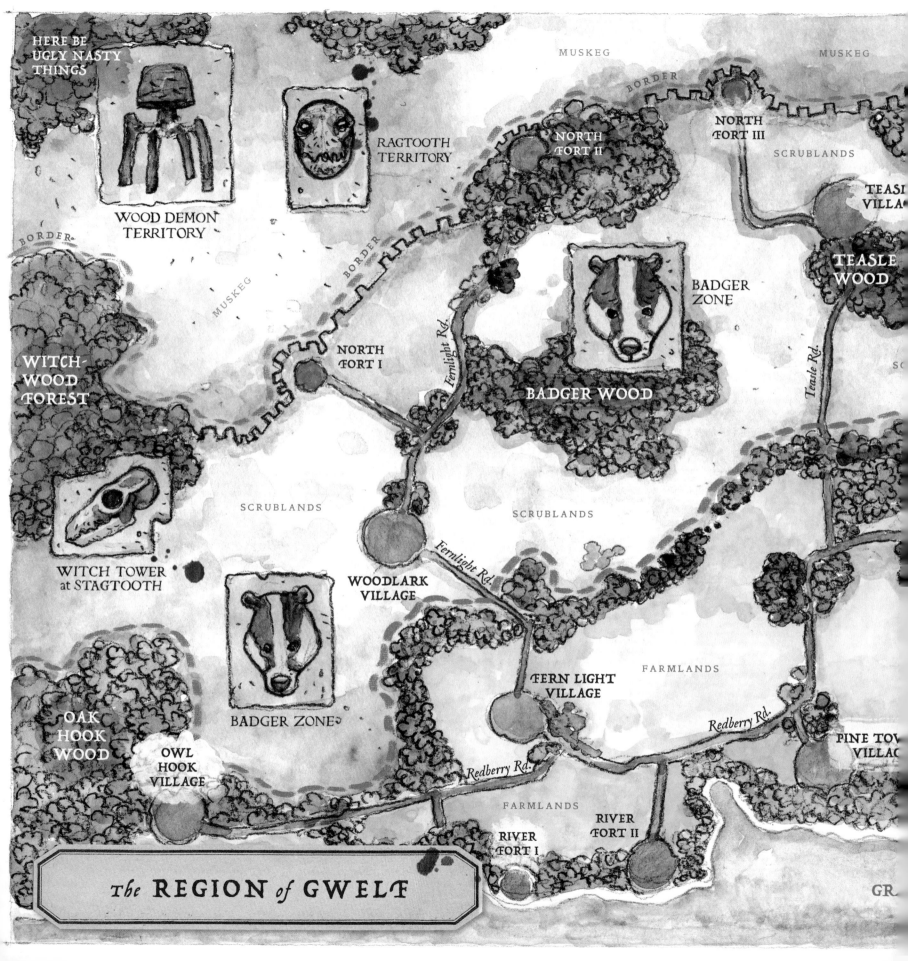

HERE BE UGLY NASTY THINGS

WOOD DEMON TERRITORY

RAGTOOTH TERRITORY

MUSKEG

MUSKEG

BORDER

NORTH FORT III

NORTH FORT II

SCRUBLANDS

TEASL VILLA

BORDER

MUSKEG

TEASLE WOOD

WITCH-WOOD FOREST

BORDER

NORTH FORT I

BADGER ZONE

BADGER WOOD

Fernlight Rd.

Teasle Rd.

WITCH TOWER at STAGTOOTH

SCRUBLANDS

SCRUBLANDS

WOODLARK VILLAGE

Fernlight Rd.

BADGER ZONE

FARMLANDS

FERN LIGHT VILLAGE

OAK HOOK WOOD

OWL HOOK VILLAGE

Redberry Rd.

PINE TOW VILLA

Redberry Rd.

FARMLANDS

RIVER FORT I

RIVER FORT II

The REGION of GWELF

GR

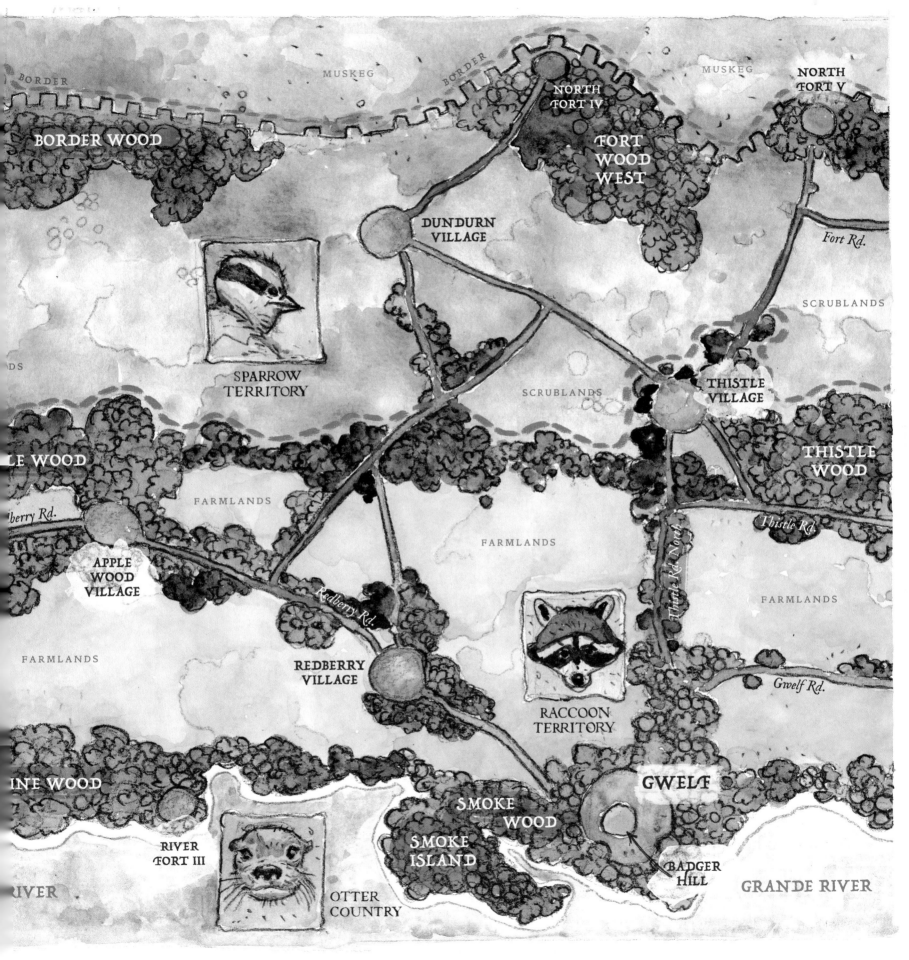

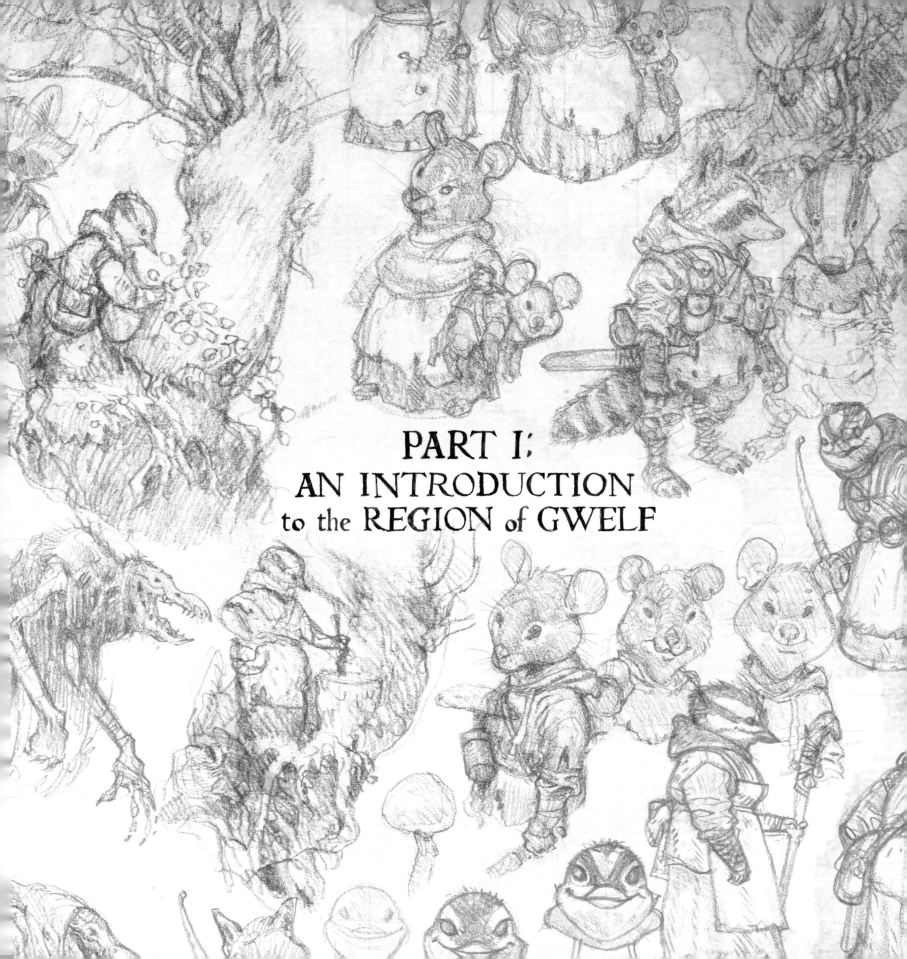

PART I:
AN INTRODUCTION
to the REGION of GWELF

Chapter 1: Preparing for the Journey

THE GREAT NORTHERN TERRITORY IS KNOWN FOR its magnificent landscapes, fascinating magics, haunt-infested regions, and stunning views of the Aurora Lights, which shine brightest in the dark of winter, the most beautiful and dangerous season in which to travel north. Much of this territory remains wild, covered in forests of enormous Smoke Pines, a thermogenic species of tree native to the area. Many who adventure into the Hinterlands beyond Gwelf do not return. This is why our first recommendation is that tourists remain within the Region of Gwelf, and within that, stick to the Farmlands and the City. The Region of Gwelf lies at the southernmost tip of the map. This is the only settled and civilized part of the territory. It is a land ruled and protected by magics and the supernatural. Gwelf is a wondrous and at times dangerous destination, offering its visitors many unusual and occasionally haunting moments. If you travel here, as with voyage into any foreign land, you must proceed with caution but will nevertheless find much to enjoy. This book will help you do just that.

The journey to the Great Northern Territory takes three days from the nearest southern city. The journey follows the main trade route across long stretches of windswept prairie and through wetlands, ending at the Grande River, which demarcates the border between the northern and southern territories. The Region of Gwelf can be reached by crossing the Grande, a deep river that spans over five hundred metres at its widest with a strong current. A boat is required, as there is no bridge. Although a seasoned adventurer might negotiate passage across on a trade boat, we recommend the ferry for tourists and larger parties. The ferry runs once a day at noon; it can also be fetched by an Otter from the Home Guard. The Otter troops protect and maintain the waterways and trade vessels and should be easy enough to hail. If it is too late to cross safely, the Guard will recommend making camp and waiting for daylight. When camping with Gwelf Otters, be sure to ask them about their adventures in the Home Guard. They may also have some crafted wares for barter or sale, as they tend to be excellent crafters and enjoy intricate work in their downtime.

Once aboard a vessel, you will soon see the City of Gwelf on the northern bank, visible through a thin fence of trees. Smoke Island, home to the Witch Market, will appear to the west once the shore is within reach. The docks of Gwelf will be ready to receive you on arrival, where you will pay your tourist tax, orient yourself, and begin your journey in Gwelf.

✳ A Note on Preparing for Your Journey

How you choose to prepare for the adventure of a lifetime depends on a number of factors. Before you set out, we urge you to read through this section of the guide and take the following into consideration: At what time of year are you planning to set out? Will you stay in the City of Gwelf, venture into the Farmlands, adventure in the Scrublands, head out towards the border, or embark into the great unknown Hinterlands? How long will you stay? Will you hire guard or guide or both?

We have provided a reference at the start of each section to guide in the selection of basic gear that you should bring if you are planning to stay any length of time in a specific area of Gwelf. Read ahead and plan accordingly.

Chapter 2: When to Visit the Region of Gwelf

Spring and Summer

WHILE GWELF CAN BE VISITED AT ANY time of the year, if you plan to make your voyage in the warmer months, aim for the Spring Equinox Festival. One of the most important celebrations in the Gwelf year, the spring equinox marks the transition from dark to light. Citizens of Gwelf celebrate the Spring Equinox Festival through rituals of renewal and celebration. Exorcists who have collected house spirits in wooden Spirit Urns over the dark winter months release the spirits, and the urns are burned in a symbolic bonfire. Houses are cleansed, pantries are emptied, and all remainders used in a large feast. While Gwelf does not offer the kinds of team sports favoured in the Southlands (excepting Otter water polo), there are a few spectator sports associated with the Spring and Autumn Equinox Festivals. Favourites include races on paw, on Pony, or in the water, as well as games of agility and Otter Aquatic Gymnastics. The latter take place most fine days along the banks of the Grande River; look for the spectator stands a league off from the point where you disembarked upon first arriving.

Summer is also a wonderful time to arrive in Gwelf. You can look forward to a long period of vacationing with a festive celebration, games, musical performances, and the traditional dramaturgy, in a region awakening to a glorious sunny season.

In the spring and summer, the atmosphere in Gwelf reflects the weather: friendly and warm. Everyone is busy, everything is fresh, everywhere is bright. The city itself is in its splendour on full, long summer days. You can view the Smoke Pines in all their magnificence, with houses built into them. Gardens, orchards, shops, and local farms are open and busy; citizens are peacefully going about their daily work, greeting friends and acquaintances, trading goods and services, or soaking up the sun on a patio. Travellers are on the road during these seasons, so inns, pubs, and teahouses are bustling. At this safe and sun-drenched time of year, visitors are welcome to explore and experience the wonders of the region. Via tours, popular walking parties, and pub crawls, visitors can experience the plethora of fine food, drink, and hospitality that Gwelf has to offer.

Autumn and Winter

The Autumn Equinox Festival is a weeklong celebration that culminates in a cleanse of Badger Hall followed by a feast and concert. Also known as the Harvest, this is when citizens prepare their homes for the coming winter with new Defensive Magics (see pages 36 and 37). An outdoor fair is part of the party, where residents can purchase items of Defensive Magics and other trinkets for themselves or as part of the customary exchange of gifts. There is also, to a lesser extent, the same set of games and competitions, and the annual "polar" swim is not to be missed, during which the daring few (not Otters) plunge into the river upon first ice sighting and try to outlast one another. A great exaggerated display is made of preparing one's home with magical decorations, and broodlings run about with brooms, "sweeping away" the dust and preparing for winter. There is much eating, drinking, and singing as everyone celebrates the last moments of frivolity before the dark winter months set in. This is by far the most anticipated party in Gwelf, said to be all the sweeter as it comes right before

the time of darkness. If you choose to stay for this celebration, be prepared to make a hasty exit before the equinox, or at the very latest before the winter solstice.

If a tourist should go beyond the limits of the City of Gwelf in autumn, they may encounter trouble in the form of haunts, wandering Mange-creatures, Rats, Ragteeth, or Ravens themselves (see pages 26 to 27). If you are of a hardier breed and thrive on adventure, extending your stay might be less daunting. Locals are always happy to have another set of paws to defend the good citizens of Gwelf against both the elements and the Ravens.

particle candle

If you choose to remain or travel in Gwelf during the dark months, we encourage you to be well supplied with as much magical protection as you can afford. Gwelf inhabitants usually remain indoors on winter evenings, attending to domestic tasks of mending, repairing, cooking, crafting, and so on. But you can be sure they will also be maintaining and improving their home defence against the Ravens and their followers. Particle candles received from the Sparrows figure prominently in their security, and there will be several burnings throughout the night. Inhabitants carve or renew runes of protection into door and window frames and attach spell ribbons to trees and fences.

If you are going to visit Gwelf in the winter as a tourist or adventurer, it is advised to stay in or make camp at night. Only the local Night Watch is out at this time, and even they would rather be home in bed. Still, overwintering in the City or Farmlands of Gwelf can certainly be a cozy experience. It can be quite comfortable to hole up at an inn for a few months if you have a manuscript to write, require a long break from your daily life, or wish to take advantage of the much lower prices offered by innkeepers and publicans at this time of the year.

Chapter 3: Inhabitants of the Region of Gwelf

From the playful Otters to the noble Sparrows, the citizens of Gwelf are a diverse mix of sizes, attitudes, appearances, and interwoven cultures. Indeed, meeting, learning from, and exchanging stories with the citizens of Gwelf is one of the primary reasons anyone might wish to travel to this wonderful region.

Citizens of Gwelf are generally a lively, hearty, and friendly lot, and any tourist should expect conversation to be quite easy and genial. Despite, or perhaps because of, the seemingly imminent danger in the region, Gwelf is a thriving community. Built into the earth, woven into the roots of the trees, and set beside the river, the City of Gwelf and the surrounding Farmlands have a cozy, pastoral atmosphere. Neighbours know one another, and in the dark of winter the whole City might show up at Badger Hall to enjoy a performance by famed musician Aspidistra Floralee Fox. This community is home to farmers who gather to celebrate new broodlings four times a year and salute fallen Home Guards twice a year (at the equinoxes), and who have worked together for generations to make Gwelf the wondrous and safe place that it is today. Gwelf offers its citizens a full life of hard work and rich culture within a tight-knit community, but it also offers a life on the edge of a frontier, something naturally adventurous and full of potential.

The citizenry of Gwelf is made up of a number of species. These are the creatures you will find living throughout the City of Gwelf, the Farmlands, and the Scrublands. We have included a small introduction to the Ravenkind creatures who make their vile homes beyond the border. These creatures are not often spotted in the City or Farmlands but venturing to the Scrublands and beyond may bring you in contact with them.

The Good-Hearted Inhabitants (Sparrowkind)

Sparrows

The Sparrows are the leadership in Gwelf. They are in tune with the magics of Gwelf, and they create and maintain the Archives, which house the wisdom and tales of Gwelf passed down through generations. They oversee the ruling and running of the institutions of Gwelf, like the Home Guard and the yearly distribution of broodlings' basic primer sets throughout the region. So, while they act in many respects like the politicians of Gwelf, they are at heart more like researchers and philosophers that have accepted the mantle of leadership.

Sparrows have been flightless since the earliest records; they have also always been crafters and users of magics. Sparrows are avid gardeners and expert botanists and have an innate understanding of their environment, lending to their knowledge and study of magics, which in Gwelf are intrinsically tied to the natural world. They comb the woods and fields for the plants, fungi, and roots they need for their admixtures, medicines, and tinctures. Sparrows also defend Gwelf from external threats by researching and developing spells that deter trespassing Ravens and unwanted haunts.

Sparrows live all across the region. Most villages and towns throughout the Farmlands and Scrublands have a de facto Sparrow leader. These individuals are more immersed in the lives of the citizenry than their more research- or magical-minded brethren, knowing every citizen in their domain by name, greeting every new broodling, and saying farewell to every departing soul. Sparrow leaders know when to perform an exorcism or call in an exorcist, how to settle minor disputes that arise between citizens, and how to shape edicts that keep everyone safe and happy.

Some Sparrows can be found in the City, supplying shops, tending to gardens, and weaving magics to ensure its stability and defence. Notably, all Sparrows congregate and share knowledge and lore periodically; travelling and City-dwelling Sparrows can nearly always be found researching or attending some meeting or conference at the Sparrow Archives. Many Sparrows, however, will choose to live a quiet life on a farmstead in or near a small community, where they can most easily commune with the land that is so integral to their magics, their knowledge, and their identity.

Blackberry and Frost mushroom tea.

It should be noted here that the Sparrows are nearly always accompanied by Mice, although the reverse could just as easily be said. Mice have become the caretakers of the Sparrows, and the Sparrows in turn are the protectors and teachers of the Mice. No other two creatures in Gwelf live in this nearly symbiotic relationship, happily serving and working with one another for survival. Even the most solitary of Sparrows is accompanied by a family of Mice.

Mice

Mice are rather inconspicuous in Gwelf. This is not generally due to reticence but more to their physical stature and the work they do. They live in the attics and basements of Sparrow cottages, establishments about the City, or else in small households burrowed into Smoke Pine roots, where they can be cozy and warm no matter the season.

The critical role that Mice play in the safety and security of Gwelf cannot be overstated. Mice work in large groups to keep the Sparrows safe, which in turn keeps Gwelf safe. It's just that simple. Sparrows are the minds that run Gwelf and make it possible for citizens to live in relative safety and comfort, and the Mice guard the Sparrows and keep them safe and comfortable. In a rare statement, Agnes Pinewreath Sparrow said: "The Mice are to us as the smoke is to the pines: naturally interconnected." To have received a comment from a Sparrow so definitive and devoid of ciphers speaks volumes of the high regard they have for their Mice compatriots.

Chances are you will not see many Mice during your stay in Gwelf. But if you should happen upon one, please be courteous and give them the respect they deserve, because they are doing work far more important and far more dangerous than you could ever imagine.

Among the Mice citizenry, abilities and skill sets vary greatly. They have created their own sort of civilization with the Sparrows that exists alongside the rest of Gwelf. It is a happy relationship that all seem to accept and enjoy. The Sparrows, in their lives full of research, magics, leadership, and defence of Gwelf, need assistance in their day-to-day dealings. The Mice provide this. Mice can be found as chefs, messengers, assistants, and business managers; they are scribes and archivists, and many dabble or become full-fledged mages in their own right, having learned it through close proximity with the texts, teachings, and activities of the Sparrows.

There are the exceptional Mice who live outside of the Sparrows' realm and run small shops in the City or have set up farmsteads of their own. These Mice are often a bit outcast, not quite belonging to the standard Sparrow-Mouse dynamic, but also not common among the other Gwelf citizenry. Finally, Mice are, as we've said, often part of the Sparrows' own personal militia, in a company called "Sparrows' Flight." The small stature of Mice makes them especially capable spies and anti-spies, and there is an elite group of the Sparrows' Flight that surreptitiously patrols Gwelf in search of Raven spies and clues to the dark magics that the Ravens use. It is only rumoured that Mice act in spy capacity, and at any rate, that is not a tourist's business.

15

Otters

Otters are likely the first Gwelf citizens you'll encounter, as they live on or near the river where you must cross to enter the Region of Gwelf. Their kinship with the water is matched only by the Badger's bond with the earth. Many Otters are in the employ of the Home Guard, working along the Grande River. Always vigilant and cunning when it comes to skirmish or ambush, the Otters are some of the most senior members of the Guard. They protect and maintain the waterways in Gwelf, from the banks of the Grande to the smaller tributaries that connect the City through the Farmlands, the Scrublands, and out to the Hinterlands. Trade in the region would not be possible without the Otters, as, whether part of the Home Guard or independent contractors, they manage all the water-faring. Otters make excellent tradescreatures or business owners, and a few Otters farm the riverbanks and riverbeds for fish and water vegetation. Otters are incredibly open and often train or take in any member of the Gwelf citizenry or alien creature who shows up adrift in their waterways. These creatures generally become masters of a typical Otter trade and are often dubbed an honorary "Otter." A notable example is Winifred Longtail, a Mouse and ferry captain. Should you board her ferry, be sure to offer her any sweet you may have brought with you, and she will regale you with fanciful river-tales in return—believe them at your own peril.

Otters are, above all else, curious and intelligent creatures. They're like the rivers, constantly tripping along in their work, or else getting into mischief. They keep themselves entertained if there isn't anything specific to do. In their downtime, Otters are expert crafters and enjoy making intricate and complicated items, both useful and frivolous.

Otter artisan crafting a piece of jewellery.

Whenever possible, an Otter will avoid direct confrontation, instead relying on traps or trickery. In conversation and relation within Gwelf society, Otters are known for their wit and their storytelling, peppering their jokes and tales with good-natured (if bawdy) humour and ridiculous puns. An Otter can be rubbed the wrong way should you forget your sense of humour, but generally Otters are well-loved and affable members of the Gwelf population. If their minds are left unengaged, an Otter can seem like a pesky prankster or a nosy neighbour, which is why there are so many busied in the ranks of the Home Guard or around card tables with Raccoons.

Foxes

Foxes are clever and creative, lovers of dramaturgy, music, and art; they can while away their hours dreaming up compositions or lazing in the summer sun, soaking up inspiration. As such, a fox will easily succumb to their lackadaisical nature if they find themselves in employment that requires menial or laborious tasks—their minds are best kept busy and in a lively environment. Foxes are practical enough to recognize that not every fox can be as talented and famous as the musician Aspidistra Floralee Fox, and so for many the arts are a hobby and a craft to be honed through journey and adventure, where their minds can be vigilant, tested, and in good company, which is likely why quite a few can be found in the Home Guard. The sense of duty and camaraderie in the Guard taps into the Fox's love for mischief and adventure, and they can often be counted on for slipping into the Hinterlands and sneaking into enemy territory on scout or skirmish missions.

Still, if there is a citizen most likely to be found hanging around the pub in the middle of the afternoon spouting sonnets or strumming a lyre, it will be a Fox. Foxes take their time learning their music, art, and craft, but they also take their time in life, laying back and enjoying themselves. They are the voyeurs of Gwelf. The creative spirit flows through them.

Musician

18

Exorcist.

For this reason, Foxes are, on occasion, adept mages. While the other creatures of Gwelf are content to use magically imbued items and rituals, a small portion of the Fox population shows an aptitude for sensing and channelling magics themselves. The creativity and freedom offered by magics often drive these remarkable individuals into the tutelage of the Sparrows, who teach and nurture the nascent magics users as they would their own Sparrow broodlings or Mouse colleagues. Assuming they have been rigorously mentored by a generous (and very patient) Sparrow, a Fox might well become adept at inscribing runes and sigils, develop new ways of laying magical traps for the enemy, and even weave music, art, and magics together to create more potent spells.

Foxes disparage any citizen who can't seem to enjoy the slice of life afforded them and so often find themselves at odds with Mice and Badgers, whose sense of duty outweighs love of independence and freedom. Still, a Fox can usually be seen among a collection of friends who can enjoy one another's company. It's as simple as that, to a Fox.

Militia

RABBITS

Rabbits possess an exceptional will to survive on the frontier and in the Farmlands of Gwelf. Their great endurance and capacity for expansion is instrumental for Gwelf as they reach out to the farthest lands to establish new farmsteads, venture up and down waterways to expand Gwelf holdings, and set up new business and trade within the region's limits. Rabbits are by far the most numerous creatures in Gwelf and are quite happy to operate in their own social circle much of the time. But among the Home Guard and during business hours, harvests, festivals, and markets, they are quite happy to engage with all of Gwelf's citizenry and are generally quite pleasant— unless you forget your manners, as you'll find that Rabbits take exception to rudeness.

Farmer

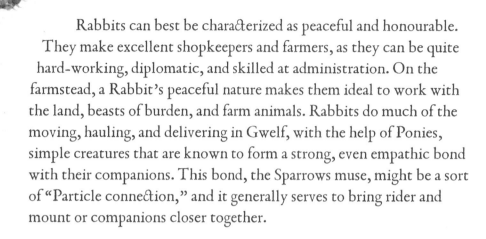

Rabbits can best be characterized as peaceful and honourable. They make excellent shopkeepers and farmers, as they can be quite hard-working, diplomatic, and skilled at administration. On the farmstead, a Rabbit's peaceful nature makes them ideal to work with the land, beasts of burden, and farm animals. Rabbits do much of the moving, hauling, and delivering in Gwelf, with the help of Ponies, simple creatures that are known to form a strong, even empathic bond with their companions. This bond, the Sparrows muse, might be a sort of "Particle connection," and it generally serves to bring rider and mount or companions closer together.

In town, a Rabbit's diplomacy and affability makes them excellent at negotiation and bartering. If a Rabbit chooses to join the Home Guard, they tend to have a very strong sense of justice and can be very aggressive in their drive to protect. They often volunteer for the dangerous mounted Home Guard and embark on hazardous duty missions, rescues, and guerrilla ambushes. In the fields of the Farmlands, the Rabbits work hard to keep Gwelf fed and supplied. Despite their drive for expansion, if given a choice, a Rabbit will likely avoid adventure and prefer to stay home with their large family or community.

Scrupulous to a fault, at times a Rabbit might look upon others as lazy or flighty, though they tend to get along quite well and can be spotted sharing a pint after work with Badgers and Foxes alike.

Badgers

Badgers are the builders and menders of Gwelf. They believe in hard work, and there is a lot for them to do, as Gwelf is ever expanding, rebuilding, and reinforcing. Badgers are one with the earth; they know silt-soil from loamy-soil by scent alone, and it is their understanding of and connection with the land and root systems that has made Gwelf the lasting and wondrous civilization that it is today. They tend not to plan their buildings before beginning them, instead trusting the very dirt and wood they work with to shape and strengthen their architecture.

Mason

They created the magnificent Sparrow Archives, an intricate building that ascends into the trees with five towering spires and descends belowground into the seven levels of archives that are kept warm and safe by the root system of an ancient Smoke Pine. Another Badger accomplishment is the famed Badger Hall. Master architect Phel Setter worked with his entire family of Badgers to build Badger Hall, a quarry emptied, entirely hollowed out, and transformed by paw into a stage and tiers of seats for spectators. It also houses over one hundred burrows to be inhabited in case of Ravenkind incursion. It is, truly, a spectacle itself, but it is mainly meant for the presentation of dramatic or musical events. It is a source of pride for all Badgers of Gwelf, and if you mention how wonderful it is, you may earn yourself a pint and some company at the pub.

Builder

Home guard

Change for Badgers happens slowly over generations. This can make Badgers seem quite stubborn and set in their ways; their unwillingness to move and bend their will is at odds with the constantly shifting earth that they revere. Nevertheless, their relentlessness can also be translated into loyalty and bravery among the ranks of the Home Guard, where many a Badger can find themselves a place to dig in—whether as smithy at an outpost or in partnership with a Pony on the mounted patrol, they will find their safe place and defend it to the last. Indeed, not all Badgers can be builders or Home Guards, but many find themselves in happy careers as independent shop-owners and entrepreneurs; the Council's own Mr. Dundill has run Root Cellar Books for over two decades after retiring from his studies with the Sparrows. Still some Badgers settle into the Farmlands and raise generations upon a single plot of land, harvesting the most sumptuous root vegetables for miles. A Badger's heart is where the home is, and there is very little that can uproot that truth.

A Badger's resolute composure can oftentimes be off-putting or even perceived as rude, but given time (and perhaps a little flattery), a Badger can be a loyal friend to the end. Any visitor would do well to bond with a Badger of Gwelf.

23

Hoteller

Raccoons

The Raccoons of Gwelf are an industrious and opportunistic lot with a business savvy to back it up. If there is a gap in the landscape of Gwelf's offerings, you can be sure a Raccoon will spot it and fill it. Do not be misled; Raccoons are hard-working creatures. Indeed, without the Raccoons there may never have been a tourism industry in Gwelf, and it might never have been comfortable for you, dear tourist or adventurer, to visit our wonderful land. Raccoon ingenuity has led to the establishment of inns, bed and breakfasts, pubs and breweries, vintners, crafts décor-shops, and tourist shops. It was their planning that led to established market days, and to date there is always a Raccoon committee involved in the planning of the equinox celebrations.

Raccoons will often join the ranks of the Home Guard as a way of seeking out adventure and opportunity. The Guard is an excellent breeding ground for connection and business entrepreneurship among the citizens of Gwelf, and there is always a Raccoon willing to put in on an endeavour and push a project forward. It was, for instance, through Raccoon insight that the Home Guard helped establish and protect the main trade routes of Gwelf. Any adventuring Home Guard company has several Raccoons in their midst, as they are clever and quick adversaries who always seem to carry the right equipment and can think on their paws. There are some Raccoons who put their minds to the study and practice of Particle or Exorcism Magics; their nimble paws and impulse for hospitality make them excellent Home Guard healers and field medics, and they can be counted on in a fix to produce the right sigil or rune to set a haunt to rest or a Rat to running.

They are much beloved in Gwelf for their easily given advice or mediation. Their witty banter, quick turns of phrase, and love of puzzles have endeared them throughout the realm of Gwelf, making them friend among all creatures. Indeed, one of the most popular books found in Gwelf is Adora Dash's *Book of Gwelf-ish Puzzles and Mazes*. You can pick up a copy in either a tourist shop or at Root Cellar Books.

Raccoons can seem overly eager and opportunistic, particularly to Rabbits, who may see them as too forward and rude. Rather, Raccoons seem especially attuned to the Otter's outlook on life and can be found brazenly betting with the water-creatures, no matter the odds.

Sommelier

25

The Boreal Inhabitants (Ravenkind)

Ragteeth

RAVENS, RAGTEETH, RATS, AND THE MANGE

Brace yourself, for now it is time to discuss the rulers of the Boreal Mountains, bringers of contagion, fear, and darkness to Gwelf, sworn enemies of the Sparrows, creators of the infernal Carrion Magics; murderers, bodysnatchers, despoilers, and destroyers, the most feared of all the inhabitants of the Great Northern Territory. After a friendly discussion of all the lovely citizens you might encounter in Gwelf, it might seem strange to devote this next section to the dark threat of the Ravens, but we feel it is necessary.

Why not address these creatures in the chapter devoted to the Hinterlands and Boreal Mountains? We thought about it, dear reader. Some thought it best that the threat of Ravens be placed at the very end so as not to scare you, and some thought it best to keep them with the magics of the land, but in the end we must admit that they are creatures of Gwelf, and so they belong here with the rest. The Raven threat is omnipresent—Ravens inevitably appear in every chapter of this book—and it is of utmost import that you know the enemy before you set paw upon the soil here. Despite our assurances in later chapters that you will be most safe in the City of Gwelf or exploring the Farmlands in the summer daylight, that safety exists only because of the extreme precautions and guardianship of the Sparrows, the Home Guard, and all the citizens of Gwelf. It is a hard-won safety that is fought for every day.

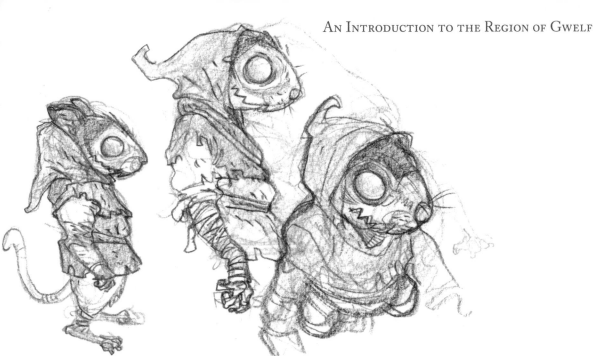

The Ravens call only one place home: the Boreal Mountains, to the far north of the territory. Capped with everlasting snow and blanketed with needle-sharp Frost Pines on their lower slopes, the Boreals look as deadly as they are. Home to avalanches and earthquakes, hauntings and Mange, the mountains are where the Ravens and their Rat and Ragteeth minions make their home. It is known that the Ravens work in tandem with the Rat population. It is suspected that the Ravens are behind the very existence of the Ragteeth. The relationship between the Ravens and their minions is not well understood, but it is thought that it might be akin to the relationship between Sparrows and Mice. It is for this reason that we simply call the inhabitants of the Boreals Ravenkind. They have built forts high in the mountains, and it is believed they must also make use of extensive cave networks inside and below the mountains. Ravens, like the Sparrows, are flightless, but any Gwelf citizen will tell you that it is most unnatural for winged creatures to dwell below ground.

We cannot say for sure what nefarious activities the Ravens engage in, up there in the Boreals. Ravens, Rats, and Ragteeth invade the peaceful Gwelf regions, they spread the Mange-disease as widely as possible, and it is believed they have a loose control over the haunts in the region as well. Reports from behind enemy lines are few and far between, and while there are no known kindly Ragteeth, there are some very few Ravens and Rats who live in the space between Ravenkind and Sparrowkind, like the dark Tinker Bands; they are "friend" to the Gwelf citizenry, and from them we have gleaned some information, which we will share in Part IV on the Scrublands and Hinterlands. What is known for certain is that there are weapons and enemy fighters flung at the Border Fort and through to Gwelf and that the Guard and citizenry are ever vigilant, for once the month of the Autumn Equinox Festival is past, Ravenkind sightings, Mange-creature incursions, and haunts flourish in ever increasing numbers.

Chapter 4: Magics

To cross the southern threshold of the Grande River is to accept an invitation to magics. Perhaps the greatest draw of the territory, aside from the call of adventure, is the magics that infuse the land and creatures. So unique and distinctly natural, the magics of Gwelf are as vital and abundant as the crisp, sweet air.

Magics flourish in many forms—some controlled, some wild. While the Sparrows are ostensibly the guardians of magics, the ones who can channel them, create them, and use them, all creatures of the territory can learn (and in rare cases even create) spells, runes, rituals, and admixtures, and they all have access to magical items. Any creature can purchase teas, candles, and talismans, or hire an exorcist to help inscribe runes of protection or expel spirits from their homes. Visitors are afforded the same luxury and can partake of magical items, rituals, and tutelage too.

The Schools of Magics

There are two main schools of magics known to Gwelf: Earth Magics and Carrion Magics. Earth Magics are the main form of magics found south of the Hinterlands. They are studied, taught, and practiced by Sparrowkind and used to heal, strengthen, and enhance the natural world and the creatures that live there. As such, they are the type of magics accessed by ordinary citizens when they employ a Particle candle, health poultice, or runic inscription. Practitioners of Earth Magics know how to gather the filaments of magics from living nature and channel them in positive ways. They can also be used defensively, to dissuade practitioners of Carrion Magics away from an area or action.

Carrion Magics are the dark opposite of Earth Magics. In a way, the two magics are each other's mirrors, drawing power from life and death. Carrion are the magics of death, certainly, but they too draw on living nature to access decay and rot. Practitioners of Carrion Magics are able to harness the shadow energy that is released as living things expire and return to the earth.

It has become the duty of Sparrows to protect the citizenry of Gwelf from the Ravens, their machinations, and their Carrion Magics. While the Sparrows do continue to practice and research Earth Magics, they also delve as much as possible into Carrion Magics. Sparrows seek to understand the ways of their nefarious brethren and believe they can uncover truths by studying the Ravenkind arts, and perhaps even gain a greater understanding of life and growth through the study of death and decay. Some Sparrows take to this avenue of study quite well, seeing the cycle of life to death within nature and the magics drawn from it as united in a perfect circle. Some have travelled rather too far down this path, as with the tragic case of Risibeth Haclaw, who was driven mad by what other Sparrows think must have been a haunt in her mind. She fled the Archives two days before the winter solstice and was never seen again.

Steam Willow

You might see examples of Carrion Magics in the Witch Market on Smoke Island or among the roving Tinker Bands. The Sparrows encourage marketgoers to dabble in this way in the hope of making new discoveries; they turn a blind eye to some questionable behaviours and objects that may be procured in the market. We advise steering clear of these artifacts, as they may be untested and unstable.

Historically, the Sparrows and Ravens were the primary scholars and practitioners of magics. At first, they worked together and supported each other in their pursuit of magical knowledge and the settlement of Gwelf, but as time passed and knowledge was gained, the differences between Sparrowkind and Ravenkind became more pronounced. Sparrows found wisdom in the magics of nature and the creation of all things, while Ravens sought out the secrets that lie in death and the truths laid to rest with the dead.

When the Ravens and Sparrows first discovered these natural magics, they practiced together in meditation. They projected their consciousnesses outside of themselves in what the Sparrows still call "Steam Consciousness," and in this state they would interact with the natural spirit world, working and exploring that realm together in pursuit of knowledge and experience. Steam Consciousness is how the original meditating Sparrows referred to the feeling when they left their bodies, like steam wisping out of a teacup, to interact with the spirits of the forest. Where the Sparrows connected with the forest spirits, or Sprites,

sprites

the Ravens were drawn to departed ancestors and disquieted spirits that seemed trapped in the realm, unable to find peace. It was only a matter of time before the natural inclinations of Sparrowkind and Ravenkind began to clash, transforming what had once been harmonious into conflict.

It was this exploration of the spirit world that drove the rift between the Sparrows and Ravens. Many hundreds of years ago, tensions rose to such a degree that factions broke out, the Ravens were on the run from the then-settlement of Gwelf, and a battle ensued at what is now called Raventag (see page 128). The Sparrows, in their fear of the Ravens' power, devised a spirit weapon that brought far more devastation than was ever intended, killing Ravenkind and Sparrowkind alike and trapping the souls of the dead upon the battlefield. Though it was a decisive victory over the Ravens, who fled into

the Boreals forever after, the catastrophic event convinced the Sparrows never to use their knowledge of the spirit realm as a weapon again. The Sparrows, with the support of the Gwelf citizenry, have branded the Ravens and their followers as witches and heretics, bodysnatchers, and necromancers, and they now choose to defeat their enemies through healing their minds, releasing their spirits, or taking away their will to fight.

After the defeat at Raventag, the Ravens too have shied away from open warfare and prefer the less costly tactics of insurgency. Thus, both sides are now stalemated and settle for skirmish and invasion along the border and into the Scrublands. Finally, it should be noted that Sparrowkind do not see Carrion Magics as being inherently evil, nor do they see Earth Magics as pure good; that is not the way of nature or of the forest Sprites with whom the Sparrows commune. Rather, magics are entropic. There are documented and labelled ways of studying and practicing magics, but there are innumerable unknowns in the Great Northern Territory; it is the hope that adventure and experience, study and experimentation will lead to differing ways of accessing, understanding, and exercising magics.

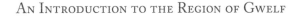

Particle candle

medicinal tinctures and particle tea blend.

PARTICLE MAGICS

If you ask a Sparrow what kind of magics they practice, they will undoubtedly call themselves "healers." Indeed, this is mainly true. The magics shared by the Sparrows are colloquially referred to as Particle Magics. Infused into the teas, medicines, poultices, and tinctures that are used for healing the ailments and emergencies of everyday Gwelf citizens, Particle Magics are also Gwelf's primary mode of defence. And when a creature is beyond the aid of these readily available medicines, a magics user can be sought out and more potent Particle Magics used to ease their suffering and make life as tolerable or even as pleasurable as possible.

Particle Magics are the most well-known manifestations of the Sparrows' Earth Magics. The Sparrows infuse their spells and magical items with the Particles they find in nature. The ingredients, herbs, minerals, pollen, roots, seeds, and so on are mixed together in sacred rituals. The magical defensive candles, incense, and tapers they make are infused with Particle Magics, which are released upon burning and stave off haunts, Mange-creatures, and other Raven machinations. The food and drink are infused with Particle Magics to make unique recipes that offer enhanced taste and health benefits. Tea is likewise infused to calm the nerves, increase creativity, promote sleep, and induce daydreaming. It is written in the histories of Sparrowkind that Particle Magics have their origins in the spirits of the forest that Sparrows first connected with through Steam Consciousness. With the aid of the spirits, the Sparrows were able to delve deeply into the art and science of Particle Magics.

iron sparrow pendant

pipe and pipe load

Blackberry and Frost mushroom tea.

33

Exorcism Magics

As a visitor from the Southlands, you have likely heard tell of the hauntings in Gwelf. The wonderful thing about stories is that there is generally a nugget of truth to them. While the tales you've heard may have been exaggerated, fabricated, or indecorous, the truth remains that there are haunts and more powerful ghosts throughout the Great Northern Territory, and so they are in Gwelf as well. For the inhabitants of the City, Farmlands, and Scrublands, these haunts, as they are more often called, are just a part of life. So too are specialized mages called "exorcists" who confront, expunge, and cleanse haunts as a day (and night) job.

In order to keep the peace between spirits and citizens, there are a great number of exorcists in Gwelf, and, while each one has their own routine and equipment for performing an exorcism, there will almost always be smoke and sound. Usually an exorcist will wear a garment glittering with natural stones pulled up from the river or smouldering with Particle incense sticks. They will jangle softly as they walk, their outfit adorned with bells made from iron or steel or bowls made from ceramic or shells. Most will be adorned with glyphs; some will have glyphs shaved into their fur, others will apply them with paint, and a few will have permanent glyph tattoos. They will bring with them an assortment of items infused with Particle Magics, generally candles, incense, tapers, and the like. Sometimes an exorcist will also set out wind chimes, singing bowls, or rattles of various materials about the space; sometimes an exorcist will simply bring their own musical instrument. Finally, if urgency allows, they will make themselves a nice cup of tea before they begin their exorcism.

The exorcist will enter a meditation trance and either summon the wind to begin whispering through the chimes and rattles or play their instrument of choice. This chaos of sound will draw out the spirit, and the smoke will make it weak and visible so that the exorcist can commune with it, banish it to its resting place, or, if need be, destroy it.

Exorcists are not typically hard to find; some of the better-known pubs and inns even retain them on staff. Any local will be able to point one out to you. Seeing an exorcism during a visit to Gwelf is a unique experience, not to be missed. A hired guide can ensure that you witness an exorcism during your visit.

Particle
Duster

Gourd smoke bomb

Protection and Defensive Magics

Like Exorcism Magics, Protection and Defensive Magics are born of the Sparrows' Earth Magics. Particle lore, herb lore, gem lore, runic knowledge, and, it is whispered, even elements of Carrion Magics are incorporated into the Defensive and Protection Magics made available to the Home Guard and the citizenry. The most common types of Defensive Magics are objects of defence (amulets and talismans) and rituals of protection (glyphs, sigils, and runes).

Objects of defence are, as their name would indicate, objects imbued with Defensive Magics. An amulet is an object that must be worn to be effective, and so amulets are usually fashioned into pendants for necklaces. Amulets are made of rocks, gems, bones, feathers, or wood and are enchanted by Sparrows to provide a specific effect as long as the amulet is worn. An amulet might provide an overall aura of health, it might bestow the benefit of trackless steps, or it might send off a current of cold to discourage haunts from selecting you as their target.

Talismans differ from amulets in two key ways. First, a talisman does not need to be worn. Rather, it should be kept accessible in a pocket or haversack so it's at paw when needed. Second, they are infused with more potent spells than an amulet, but once used lay dormant until reimbued. When activated with a keyword or gesture, a talisman might create a flash of light that stuns haunts or Mange-creatures, release a spellsong to confuse or daze an enemy, or send a message for aid to your nearest ally.

The rituals of protection can be broken down into three. The first, glyphs, are ideograms imbued with magical meaning and placed directly upon the body. Temporary glyphs might be dyed onto or shaved into fur or feathers, while permanent glyphs might be tattooed onto a creature's body. Glyphs are derived from the Sparrows' natural philosophy, representing ideas of nature, life, and growth in small, easy-to-draw images. For example, a glyph drawn in a series of jagged peaks with a bar drawn through represents the Boreal Mountains and offers some protection by rebuffing creatures native to the mountain region, such as Mange-creatures. Glyphs are found to be most effective for living creatures rather than for property, because they derive their strength from the magics of the living world.

Storm
Candle

Smoker

Recorder

A sigil is similar to a glyph but is drawn, burned, carved, or otherwise inscribed onto an inanimate object. Sigils come from the alchemical alphabet and imbue the objects with protections against theft, breakage, and weakness. Stronger sigils might cause belongings to turn to ash if they fall into enemy claws or burn thieving claws with magics. If you are setting out from the City of Gwelf for any reason at any time of year, you would be wise to get your shoes, haversack, and walking stick inscribed with sigils. These sigils lose power over time and can be renewed at the Sparrow Market in the City, at the Witch Market, by any Sparrow or mage of decent aptitude, or by the Tinkers if you happen to be on the road.

A rune is location-specific Protection Magics. Rooted in deep, elemental Earth Magics and drawn from the rocks and roots, runes connect a built location (though a campsite may benefit from runes as well) with the surrounding natural environment. They are powerful protection and prevent Ravens, Mange-creatures, and haunts from creeping through a door or window. Citizens of Gwelf have runes carved and renewed at least twice a year to protect their homes, businesses, and other shared spaces.

Finally, while most of these magics are defensive, some slightly more offensive magics are employed by the Home Guard and adventurers. Not only are there generally a good number of exorcists and mages in the Guard, but the Sparrows and their disciples also produce some weapons against incursions. To discourage vandals, for example, a Home Guard might set a MisMind Trap, which, when triggered, will leave the trap-tripper confused and of the impression that they need to return home. The Guard also makes frequent use of Particle cannons, Stonk, grenades, and Particle-infused war bows (see page 136).

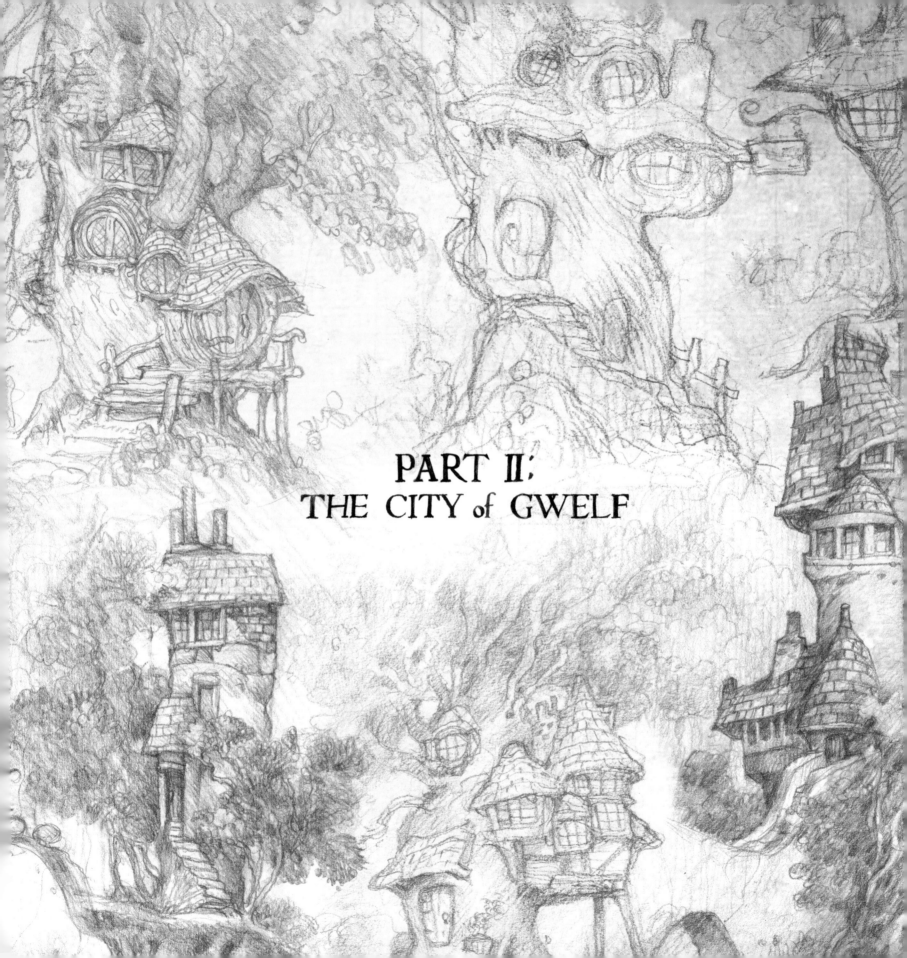

PART II:
THE CITY of GWELF

Chapter 5: Overview of the City of Gwelf

ONCE YOU HAVE REACHED THE NORTHERN BANK of the Grande River, you will be within the limits of the City of Gwelf, capital of the region. All of the trade and business and much of the cultural entertainment that happens in the territory is here. It is the perfect launching point for vacation or adventure, and no matter your hurry, there are a few must-see places here.

Upon arrival, be ready to give your name, occupation, and origin at the Home Guard Office. You will be asked to pay a tourist tax; this is a nominal fee and an important part of Gwelf's economy, allowing Gwelf to welcome travellers from near and far to a safe, clean, and whimsical place filled with exciting experiences. While the tax must be paid in gold, in the City you can use coin or barter with citizens if you have a skill or commodity you can trade.

From the shore, follow the beaten path along the river towards the City. You will see a forest of ancient trees rising before you: that is the City of Gwelf.

List of Equipment

The list that follows is a guide for all those who plan to visit the City:

— A haversack full of daily essentials
— Some coins to cross the river, hire a guide, and sit in a pub
— Good boots
— A journal or a good book
— A knife

Planning Your Visit

It is difficult to suggest how long you should stay in the City of Gwelf; as often as not, the plan for a four-day getaway or a two-week exploration turns into a two-month stay. Best to come prepared!

There are typically two ways a traveller might start their day in the City of Gwelf. The early riser will be up with the Sparrows to hear them sing greetings to the morning and watch the sun rise. This will allow you to secure your favourite spot in the dining room of your inn, leaving the table wide open in invitation for others to join you or burying your nose in a book or a journal as a gentle request to be left to yourself. The later riser can arrange for a tray to be left at their door and will awaken at their chosen hour to the smell of fresh-cooked breakfast and the hot, fortifying tea of their choice enticing them awake.

Either way, once you've breakfasted in bed or in the dining room, it is time to start your day. If you are the gregarious type who wishes to let their paws take them where they may, then it's time to head out the door and follow the sound of adventure. If you are a more cautious or organized sort, then it is time to hire a guide (see page 46).

Though the capital isn't as large as most Southland metropolises, you will find yourself endlessly fascinated by the shops, the experiences, the citizens, the architecture, the performances, the food, and the nature surrounding it all. To get an idea of how long you might spend in a particular place, it is best to have a chat with your guide, the innkeeper, and your fellow patrons. If you are a reader, for example, you'll want to budget a whole day to Root Cellar Books, and another to the Sparrow Archives.
If you are visiting to learn about the magics of Gwelf, you'll want those same two days plus another for the magics shops in the City and at least one evening spent in the Witch Market. You may also wish to view an exorcism, a Sparrow imbuing artifacts, and one of our more famed magical, musical, or theatrical performances. In any case, on with your good walking boots and your amulet of protection, and out the door you go.

43

A Word about Haunts and Wintertime

Haunts are an everyday part of life in Gwelf. Though the capital city is the safest place you can be in terms of the Raven threat, it is also somewhat ironically one of the most haunted places. The most powerful trick Ravenkind possesses is their ability to manipulate the afterlife. As the Sparrows have known for decades, if a creature is killed by a Raven weapon, their spirit will remain trapped as a haunt. By now the entire Region of Gwelf is haunted by ghosts of varying power and malevolence. The Sparrows are still trying to unravel this mystery, working with exorcism specialists and studying what is known of haunts and Carrion Magics, but it appears the manner of one's death and the magics used will determine the essential nastiness of the subsequent haunt. The haunts in an urban area, as a general rule, don't seem to be as effective or lingering as the ones found farther out. The closer you are to the border, the worse the haunts become, but even affable haunts can be annoying with their howling and moaning, knocking things over and bringing with them an unshakeable chill. They need to be helped onward, to let go of their existence on the earthly plane. Haunts seek out warmth and company. They congregate around campfires, Tinker Band camps, markets, inns, and pubs. These incorporeal creatures can be found in the City of Gwelf at any time but particularly at night and in winter, when they seek out the warmth of the Smoke Pines and the City's hearths. The citizens generally keep them out of their homes with various Particle Magics defences and exorcists.

All pubs, inns, and businesses that are open late will have protective candles and incense lit every single night, no matter the season. The very warmth of the Smoke Pines is often enough to keep Ravenkind invaders at bay, but of late, along with the haunts, the Mange-creatures have been wandering into the City in the dead of winter—it seems they are drawn to the warmth and light of civilization. A visitor should be aware that this is a wintertime hazard and that if they are out and enjoying the nightlife, they should have a companion at their side at all times. And no matter the time of year, as you return to your inn, tired but happy from your day's journeys, light a Particle candle. It's good practice, and there is nothing friendlier than the sight of all the candles bobbing along, offering protection and light as night settles in.

Guides In and Out of the City

Guides in the City of Gwelf are quite easily obtained. Simply pop into a tea shop or a pub; there are nearly always tables dedicated to this lot, and you should feel free to approach them and begin negotiations.

If you plan to visit the City during one of the festivals, then we recommend you send word at least a few months ahead of your visit, both to book a room and to secure the services of a guide. Include a coin or two for both the room and the guide, and mention the name of your preferred lodgings, if you have them, and also the name of your guide, if one is known to you. The workers of Gwelf are honest folk, and you can rest assured that this deposit will ensure the services you require are awaiting you.

While not absolutely necessary in the City itself, many first-time visitors still greatly benefit from hiring a guide for at least a day or two to help them sort out the maps, find the best spots to eat and drink, and take day trips out to the landmarks around the City. They will explain to you how the magics of the City work, help you with Particle candles and protections, and introduce you to some of the best-known friendly faces. Especially during the autumn and, if you insist on staying, in the winter, a guide is essential to teach you how to stay safe. A guide will show you how to use a knife or hire a guard, find a Sparrow and request their services, have sigils inscribed on belongings, and much more. If you are planning to venture beyond the confines of the City, then a guide is essential on your first trip. Many a traveller has thought they can make it out to the Pine Cone Inn in the Farmlands without worry only to find themselves lost in a briar patch or in need of rescue.

We can only stress that hiring a guide is a wise decision. Even if you only need one for a day or two to find your paws, your experience will be all the richer for it.

46

Chapter 6: Entertainment in the City of Gwelf

Music

MUSIC IS AN INTEGRAL PART OF GWELF culture. Indeed, it is unlikely that you will leave the City without having heard music and song nearly every day. The Sparrows study music because it is an integral part of their magics, the Foxes enjoy the artistry of it, and the rest of the citizenry enjoy the craft and entertainment of it. Some musicians apprentice with exceptional and famous Gwelf citizens, or else study closely with the Sparrows to develop music spells. These musical mages are generally Fox masters who have been Sparrow trained; they are the bards, composers, and musicians. They may also become exorcists who will use their music in a more performative way during the expulsion of haunts. Their music spells can also be powerful against Ravenkind, if used correctly. Likewise, the Sparrow Songster Society, in which Sparrows gather to sing traditional magical and mundane songs based on the complex birdsong of the territory, infuse their songs with magics to uplift the spirit, leaving the listener feeling light and carefree. The music in Gwelf can be beautiful or dangerous, depending on who is playing and who is listening, but it is often also simply an enjoyment.

Most inns and taverns will have a schedule of performers for your enjoyment, and there are nightly performances at Badger Hall in spring and summer that drop down to weekly in the fall and monthly in the winter. While these winter performances are only four or five in number, they are all held in Badger Hall, which is packed

with nearly every citizen of the City of Gwelf; many visitors from the surrounding areas make the trek in, and tourists are always welcome. These over-attended performances are so filled with warmth and the sound of music and magics that, if you do overwinter in Gwelf, it is an experience not to be missed.

Theatre

If you enjoy theatre, then a visit to the Brambleberry Commons is a must. This wonderful open-air theatre in the heart of the City operates spring, summer, and fall with short comedic performances reserved for lunchtime viewing in the summer and autumn and longer dramatic and musical productions for spring. Several troupes share the space, carefully coordinating their offerings to avoid double-booking or accidentally mounting the same production, as happened one memorable year when the Broodling's Chorus and the Senior Rabbits' Thespianical Association both put on very different versions of the Tale of Elias Thumper the Bloody—though, to be fair, it was actually quite worth seeing both productions on consecutive evenings.

Games

There are also numerous games of chance all throughout the region. Backgammon, dice, and card games are all favourites, and you can usually entice a new friend into a game of riddles, craps, or whist. The Sparrows greatly favour a Gwelf variation on chess, in which the southern bishops are replaced with Sparrow and Raven figures who are able to move in runic patterns to block each other and enchant their opponent's pieces.

Chapter 7: Where to Stay in the City

The Belle Flower Inn

THE LARGEST AND MOST RECOMMENDED SPOT TO rest your head in Gwelf is the Belle Flower Inn. This wonderful inn is also the oldest in the City, and it has been in the same family for over five hundred years. Built directly into an ancient, enchanted cherry tree, it gets its name from the beautiful flowers that blossom all spring and summer long. The inn is always expanding, slowly adding rooms as the tree grows ever taller and wider. This charming inn boasts soft beds, stunning views from every room, and easy access to all the amenities of the City, since it's located in the main square. Many a City guide stops by to break their fast here, both because the food is first rate and because they like to be available for hire to new arrivals.

You'll want to visit the Visitors' Library on the main floor of the inn, whether you're staying here or not. Open to the public, the library boasts books left by visitors to Gwelf, who are encouraged to leave the books they brought with them here. Many visitors will send a copy of their books of art, poetry, and stories inspired by their time in Gwelf back to the Belle Flower. It is a wonderful way to experience Gwelf both as a citizen and a visitor, to read through or gaze upon the way visitors experience the region.

An important landmark, the Belle Flower is owned by the Council, but don't imagine that our involvement in this guidebook has swayed our reportage in any way! The Belle Flower is such a large business that it has separate proprietors for the hotel, the restaurant, and the tearoom. The current tearoom proprietor of the Belle Flower is the celebrated tea sommelier Chamberlain Sun Mouse. Mice, as you might be aware, very rarely hold such positions, preferring instead to hire themselves out to Sparrows and work in close kinship with our magical protectors. But of course, one's species does not dictate one's destiny!

The Haunt Inn

It will likely not surprise you to learn that this inn, built into a gnarled old oak tree, claims to be the most haunted place in the City. Whether that's true is up for debate, but it certainly is home to its share of haunts. No one is sure why they are continually drawn to the inn. Some say the owners procure "ghost lures" from the Witch Market. Others say that family and friends promise to stay at the inn after they're gone, which makes for an everchanging cast of ghostly characters showing up to knock on windows, blow out candles, or tie shoelaces together.

While this might not be to everyone's taste, it's certainly a unique experience and one you'll be talking about long after you leave. The owner, Mr. Benedict B. Baskins, Raccoon, is a veritable font of knowledge on all things ghostly. While not an exorcist himself, Mr. Baskins is considered a living archive of theoretical knowledge. Ask him anything about rituals, herbs, gemstones, and Exorcism Magics, and he'll tell you. Exorcists often come to him for advice and can often be seen sharing a glass of stout with him on an afternoon as they talk over their latest experiences.

Bed and Breakfasts

Gwelf is also home to any number of bed and breakfasts. These often come and go depending on the season. Some proprietors have a fluctuating number of rooms in any given season (for instance, winter sees fewer rooms as a result of the need for heat and protection), and innkeepers may travel and close shop or offer more limited services. For the festivals, many citizens open their homes and barn lofts to earn a few extra coins. This is all to say that a comprehensive list is not an easy thing to create, especially to be published in a book that we hope will last for many years to come. If you wish to stay in a bed and breakfast, which tends to be an altogether quieter and more economical option than the larger inns, simply ask at the Home Guard Office on your way into the City for a recommendation, and someone will send you to the right place.

A full breakfast

Chapter 8: Where to Eat in the City

TEA, ALE ON A PATIO, MUSIC, AND conversation are central to life in Gwelf. The tea in Gwelf is an attraction for all. If you are feeling tired, anxious, or upset, teas can lift your spirits with their special herbal blends; infused with Particle Magics, these teas are sure to bring a sense of calm and ease to your spirit. A good cup of tea will make your visit to Gwelf complete.

Pubs are also a favourite. Gwelf is known for both its wide variety of ales, meads, and liquors and its live music. Just about everyone turns up at the pub sooner or later. Conversation is where fast friends are made with stories to trade. It is how the inhabitants of the territory hear tell of the outside world and share their own experiences with visitors. There are so many different teas and brews available in the City, and many a fine folk live a simple life, lingering over their favourite drink in their favourite teahouse or tavern after a good day working the land, plying their wares, or keeping the citizenry safe.

The Rose and Nettle Teahouse

We also recommend popping into the Rose and Nettle for a nice cup of tea in the afternoon.
This lovely teahouse is the choice for any special occasion and a must for visitors. The afternoon tea
service at the Rose and Nettle can last for three hours, with a perfectly dizzying array of sweets, finger
sandwiches, miniature mousses, fruits, and scones, each arriving with its own tea pairing. You can
request your teas or place yourself in the paws of Madame Camilla, a Rabbit with a nose for fine tea.
This tea sommelier has an uncanny knack for picking out exactly the flavours you didn't know you
most wanted.

The Rose and Nettle also offers teas that can be bought in bulk and brought home, as well as
steaming cups that can be enjoyed on their own, without the full afternoon tea treatment. Beware,
though: tea in Gwelf is not like what you might drink in the Southlands. When visiting, be sure not to
overindulge in your tea. For instance, of the nettle brew, for creativity, only two cups are recommended
at a time, lest delusions set in. Also available are curative teas, like those for arthritis or rheumatism,
and those that induce a meditative trance, which are more often used by exorcists in their studies or
activities in the spirit realm. Each will come with a recommended dosage from Madame Camilla,
and you would be best served heeding her advice.

Treetop Public House

The most family friendly of the City's pubs, this sister establishment to the Belle Flower Inn is built into the upper branches of the cherry that is home to the inn. This means that every few years, an industrious crew of Badgers and Raccoons dismantles the pub wholesale and moves it up into the newer branches. This ensures that the Treetop always lives up to its name and affords the best view in the whole City. Sharing a similar sensibility—and the same kitchen—as the Belle Flower's tearoom, the Treetop offers a hearty menu meant to sate the body and the soul. The pub's twice-fried fingerling potatoes are the stuff of legend, and they offer as many flavours of juices for broodlings as ales and liquors for grown citizens.

The Fireside Pub

Locals claim you haven't lived until you've tasted the mussel stew paired with a pint of the finest local barley beer here. True to its name, the entire restaurant is built around a massive circular fireplace carved into an ancient petrified Smoke Pine. Every seat is a fireside seat. The Fireside is a particular favourite in autumn, when the fire crackles merrily all night long; even in summer they keep the embers glowing, and it's always comfortable.

The Baddington Arms

The Baddington Arms was so named by the Badger Vega Baddington in honour of Old Grandpa Baddington, a longstanding member of the Night Watch. A favourite spot of Night Watch members, it opens at dusk and closes a little after dawn, serving a complimentary breakfast to any Night Watch members coming off their patrol. It is also a great place to strike up some of the most interesting conversations and hear some of the most interesting stories you will get in the City. The Night Watch, current and retired, can tell you harrowing tales from the frontlines of the war against Ravenkind.

Heavily warded with runes and Defensive Magics, this pub boasts "nap nooks" for anyone who has stayed too long and had a pint or two too many to safely embark on the journey home. For an extra silver, you'll be given a comfortable blanket, a lavender-filled pillow, and the promise of a good strong tea in the morning.

Chapter 9:
Where to Shop in the City

THE CITY OF GWELF MIGHT BE SMALL geographically, but it is jam-packed with places to visit. There are fascinating day trips to be made out to our storied landmarks, walking paths to trip along, and, of course, shopping to be done.

Every trip to Gwelf should begin with a shopping trip in the City. For leisurely visitors, there are plenty of souvenirs unique to the region. Explore the Sparrow or Witch Market (with proper guidance, of course) and purchase some homespun cloth, pawcrafted wind chimes, and chandler-made candles and incense. If you are an art collector, be sure to make time to commission a custom piece for yourself or as a gift so you can take some of Gwelf home with you. For the more adventurous tourist, we also recommend beginning your journey with a shopping trip so that you might be equipped for any eventuality to be had in the region. If you didn't bring them, be sure to pick up a sturdy backpack and cobbler-made boots (see Paws and Claws Cobblers, page 70), stock up on Particle candles, and invest in protection amulets. If you are proficient, be sure to arm and armour yourself as well.

Branching off from the main square, where the Belle Flower Inn is located, you will find a number of streets that are home to merchants, craftscreatures, and markets. It's a bustling downtown experience. You will be reminded every time you step out onto the warm streets at any time of year that much of the City is built into the root systems of Smoke Pines and kept heated by these thermogenic trees. The main thoroughfares that branch off from the square are the Particulate, High Street, the Forges, and the Avenue of Artists. The more you wander, the more side streets and hidden paths you will uncover, and we can guarantee that each will have at least one interesting shop, tearoom, or café to delight you. Use the following as a guide to begin your exploration of the City, but, especially in daylight, don't be afraid to step off the main path and uncover other wonders.

The Particulate

Along this winding street you will find magics shops where magical defences, mostly Particle Magics in nature, can be purchased. This is the place to purchase infusion candles and incense to burn at night to keep Ravenkind away. Citizens will purchase amulets, hire a craftscreature to carve runes on the outside of their lintels or paint them onto their house walls, shave runic tattoos into their fur, or reimbue magical artifacts.

Common door runes of warding and protection

SPARROW MARKET

We strongly advise all visitors to make this their first stop after securing a place to rest their heads for the night and hiring a guide if one is desired. The Sparrow Market is a gorgeous arboreal market that takes up most of the length of the Particulate, high up in the treetops. Most of the shops along the street are built into the trunks of trees, and the Sparrow Market is built into their branches in a delicate, highly engineered network of nestlike shops and stalls. A number of trees with pawholds or hidden ladders can be found if you know where to look along the street. If you hire a guide, they will bring you into the market and ensure you visit all the most interesting stalls. You will find Sparrows to enchant amulets for you, paint or shave glyphs into your fur, and emblazon sigils onto your belongings. Any of these Defensive Magics are a wise investment if you plan to travel to the Farmlands and beyond; if you plan to be anywhere in the region during the autumn or winter, then it becomes not simply wise but essential for your safety. While you can always find a Sparrow who will carve protective runes into your doorway, more Sparrows make the journey to the City in the early autumn to perform this service, as this is when the bulk of the citizenry renew the protective runes on their homes and businesses.

You will also find stalls where herbal tinctures and remedies are sold, where medicinal and magical teas can be purchased, and where specialized Particle candles and incenses may be commissioned. If you spot a Mouse anywhere, it will most certainly be here, selling and delivering wares on behalf of the Sparrows. You will likely spend a whole day exploring the Sparrow Market; don't be surprised if you find yourself drawn back again and again to discover new stalls and magical products for purchase.

63

High Street

As the name suggests, this street is
semi-arboreal, and it is where you can shop for
goods in Gwelf. A number of wonderful shops have
called High Street home for decades.

THE PRINT SHOP

At the crossroads of the Particulate and High Street, you will find the Print Shop, home to the largest
and oldest continually running printing press. It is the only print shop in the territory, although there are
other printing presses scattered across the region. While many of the Sparrows still prefer to scribe their
writings, most of the books in Gwelf are printed in this very shop. At the very least, the shop runs weekly
to ensure the City's newspaper, the *Gwelf Daily Acorn*, is fresh and pressed before daybreak.

Owned by the City of Gwelf, the shop is currently overseen by Councilmember Loquacious
Bailey Raccoon, a brilliant entrepreneur, typesetter, and organizational mastermind who maintains the
rigorous schedule that allows all the work to get done. The citizenry makes good use of the enchanted
printing presses. Using what they call a simple duplication spell, the Sparrows are able to set the type
on one press and have the other presses immediately mimic the typesetting and print identical pages.
This allows for mass production of printed materials in short order.

The shop employs a number of bookbinders as well. Visitors are welcome to come and watch
different aspects of the process. If you have good timing and a bit of luck, you might also get to see how
magical books are bound. While the more arcane and complex magical texts may exist in only one or
two paw-scribed copies squirrelled away in Sparrow homes, other treatises for lesser magics workers or
interested creatures are often produced in multiple copies at the Print Shop. Magical tomes are infused
with Particle Magics for a number of reasons, including to enhance the memory of the reader, who will
better retain the information in these books, and to protect against evil eyes by warding against any
practitioner of Carrion Magics.

Beside the Print Shop is a café called the Scriptorium, where the scribes of the City like to gather.
For those who have had an adventure in Gwelf, it is a common practice to hire a scribe. This way, you
can share your story to be entered into the annals of the territory's history. Have a copy printed for the
Sparrow Archives, a copy for the Visitors' Library at the Belle Flower, and a copy for your own library
for a truly unique souvenir of your time in Gwelf. You might also book a time with Loquacious to print
your own materials while you are in the City. Many a visitor planning to venture farther afield will print
leaflets seeking travel companions.

Root Cellar Books

Directly across the street from the Print Shop is Root Cellar Books. The bookstore is an old establishment run by our own Mr. Dundill. It's built into the root system of a large Smoke Pine, and the majority of the books are supplied by the Sparrows via the Print Shop, but some books are scribed for resale here as well. There are plenty of unique, eccentric books written and illustrated by citizens that have imbibed lots of tea, a few more famous historical and geographical texts, music, poetry, epic tales, and the like, and still a few more on the basic magics of Gwelf written mainly by Sparrows. Broodlings' basic primer sets are also always available. Every citizen in Gwelf is literate at least at a basic level, and these sets are created and distributed by the Sparrows for a nominal fee.

One set can be reused within one family several times or shared by neighbours; it can make a lovely keepsake for little ones back home.

Mr. Dundill was once an apprentice at the Sparrow Archives; though Badgers are not traditionally magics users, these stalwart creatures are excellent scholars if a particular subject catches their attention. Mr. Dundill is one such scholar. He spent many happy years among the books and scrolls and secrets of the Archives. He left the Archives and set up his book shop, nestled among the Smoke Pine root system of the City, with hopes of a life of laughter and conversation with the citizenry and tourists of Gwelf. With the excellent relationship between himself and the Sparrows, Mr. Dundill ensures that a copy of every book that passes through his shop also finds a home in the Archives, thus contributing to a continuous and ever-growing bastion of knowledge in the territory.

No matter what you are looking for, Mr. Dundill will blow the dust off the books for you and find it. If there is any research you want to do in Gwelf, this is the place to start. And if your research takes you to the Sparrow Archives, Mr. Dundill will write you a letter of recommendation to gain you admittance.

Root Cellar Books also has a fine selection of stationery. You will find homemade paper and sturdy parchment, sketchbooks, and journals, as well as quills, inks, charcoals, pastels, and watercolours.

BAILIWICK CANDLE SHOPPE

Candles and the like are basic self-defence in Gwelf,
so it's a good idea to stock up as needed for your planned adventures.
We recommend the Bailiwick Candle Shoppe to get you started. Jay Bailiwick is an enduring
Sparrow in the community. Having spent many years studying in the Sparrow Archives, he then
decided he wanted to explore Gwelf and actively help in the battle against Ravenkind. Thus,
he embarked upon a tour of Gwelf, visiting particularly haunted buildings and woods, learning
alongside exorcists, and joining the Home Guard in the Scrublands and along the border.

Protection

Calming

Warmth

Long burning

Rather than designing a grand weapon or burying himself in magical research, Mr. Bailiwick found that the most pressing need for his skills and knowledge was accessible magics for inhabitants across the territory. It was all well and good for the Home Guard to have enchanted arrows and Particle incense bombs. It was quite another for the everyday citizen trying to get home from selling their wares at the market, or visiting a relative and being caught out on the dark road alone, or facing the horror of a Mange-creature shambling into their home. So Mr. Bailiwick created a comprehensive inventory of candles and incense that common creatures might need throughout the year and began to sell and ship these items from the Shoppe.

Haunt

Warding

Sleep

The Farmers' Market

While many inhabitants of the City have their own gardens, the bulk of the food produced in Gwelf comes from the Farmlands (see page 83). And so, while a family might grow their favourite peas and edible flowers at home or on their balcony, many citizens shop at the Farmers' Market, which has a steady stream of fresh goods arriving daily. If you do not plan to make the trip to the Farmlands yourself, you can get a taste of it here at the Farmers' Market. Along with fruits, vegetables, and grains, you will find breads, cheeses, fishes, preserves, honeys, juices, and everyday teas among the everchanging stock. Before you embark on a journey, be it a day trip or out into the far reaches of the territory, fill your haversack with the hearty, healthy foods of the region here at the market.

PAWS AND CLAWS COBBLER

While there are other cobblers who can be hired, Paws and Claws is the best known and has the most ready-to-wear options fit for the paw of any good creature of Gwelf. Dash Kitsey, "Kits," comes from a long line of cobblers and, with a fine eye for fashion, she can provide you with a dazzling selection of pawwear tailored to fit just right. If you are planning on doing any sort of walking, and indeed if you are going to head out to the Farmlands and beyond, be sure to hire a cobbler or simply stop in at Paws and Claws to have a pair of sturdy boots made.

Also note—if you are one of those brave souls whose journey will take them out into the Scrublands and beyond, be sure to have your boots enchanted at the Sparrow or Witch Market before you embark on your adventure. Every spell counts.

ADVENTURE OUTFITTING

For the shopper who is looking for more than a pretty dress or comfortable trouser, visit this shop at the intersection of High Street and the Forges. Adventure Outfitting provides heavy-duty clothing, haversacks, tents, tarpaulins, ropes, walking sticks, knives, and other gear for adventurers. Don't embark on a camping trip, a journey into the Farmlands and beyond, or an autumnal exploration without stocking up here first. The shop offers clothing and gear with basic defensive enchantments; deals can be struck whereby mages who are affiliated with the shop will offer more personalized or heavier protections on items purchased here at a discount.

The Forges

This long street is called the Forges in homage to the many smiths and armourers who have set up shop here. Though Gwelf is a peaceful territory with strong border relations to the south, there is nonetheless good reason for an entire section of the shopping district to be devoted to arms and armaments. Defensive and offensive weaponry is a necessity for any inhabitant of or visitor to Gwelf, especially those venturing out at night, in winter, or into the farther, wilder reaches of the land.

THE GUILD OF SMITHS

Smiths in Gwelf are primarily Badgers, though other creatures can occasionally be found working the forges. Only smiths are allowed inside the headquarters, where it is said apprentices begin their training. Here, texts on smithing history, techniques, and lore can be found, though it should be noted that the secrets of the smiths are carefully guarded. It is also said that a small brewery is located inside the headquarters that produces the finest stout in all the land, but only smiths are allowed to drink there.

A number of independent smiths can be found all along the Forges, spreading out from headquarters. Smiths make Pony shoes, farming implements, kitchenware, tools, nails, and decorative ironwork. However, most smiths, no matter their medium, will take commissions. If you will be in the City long enough or are planning to return the next season or year to pick up your purchase, then putting in an order for a one-of-a-kind item might be an option for you. You can visit specialized armourers who forge swords, daggers, knives, shields, and armour for creatures of all shapes and sizes, skills, and strengths. From light, breathable summer armour to heavy rust-proof winter mail, you will be in good paws with a member of the Guild.

THE STRAIGHT ARROW

The bow is perhaps the most common weapon in the Home Guard beyond the Farmlands, allowing for ranged attacks, coordinated offensives, and magical enhancements. The Straight Arrow is a collective of bowyers and fletchers run by council member Toffee Bryndon Rabbit. With several locations (you will find several Straight Arrow outposts in the Farmlands and Scrublands), these makers provide a comprehensive array of ranged weaponry. Master bowyers create shortbows, longbows, and crossbows from yew, maple, oak, and even Smoke Pine.

71

The fletchers, who are primarily Mice, work with Sparrows to notch bolts and arrows with fine Sparrow feathers and enchantments to allow for better aim, longer range, and delivery of Particle Magics, including fire and smoke bombardment, Particle bursts, and jets of cold. They also tip the bolts and arrows with a variety of materials, including copper, stone, precious gems, and bone.

The rarest of all arrows is fletched with Sparrow feathers and tipped with Raven bones, which have a kind of critical effect on Ravenkind, inflicting more damage than any other known substance. A favourite stop for tourists, you can arrange to take an introductory lesson on the archery range behind the shop. Broodlings and youths of Gwelf often take lessons all spring and summer long, and you will find many fine archers in the region because of it.

HEARTWOOD CARPENTRY

This collective is where almost all the carpenters, architects, furniture makers, and cabinetmakers of Gwelf have membership. No one craftscreature owns Heartwood Carpentry. Instead, it operates rather like the Smiths' Guild, providing fair wages to its artisans, schooling, a place of belonging, good wages, and guaranteed work to the membership.

In the showroom, you may peruse and purchase bookcases and hearths, bowls and utensils, gardening tools and walking sticks, as well as pieces of furniture. Heartwood is known for its beautiful bentwood rocking chairs, crafted of finest Smoke Pine and providing a constant source of warmth and comfort. Examples of cabinetry and doorways as well as portfolios of larger projects, including homes and businesses, can be found in the showroom.

Avenue of Artists

This magical collective of artists of all stripes is, for some, the main reason to journey to Gwelf. Art from all over Gwelf can be found here. Artists are everchanging, and it's not uncommon for an artist to rent a stall for a week, sell all their wares, and then head home with heavy pockets. Indeed, this is a favourite spot to shop for many citizens because of the constantly changing goods that can be purchased here.

Art in Gwelf is vast and varying, but there are many painters, carvers, dyers, tinkers, tailors, writers, poets, and musicians. You will find buskers here, and they will usually be spaced out respectfully so as not to interfere with one another's tunes or recitations. Some will have instruments for sale for visitors such as yourself. Toss a coin into their hat or instrument case and enjoy the fine entertainment of the Region of Gwelf; visit artists, request commissions, and return home with wondrous gifts.

Smoke Island

Finally, we recommend a visit to Smoke Island. The largest island in the region, covering more area than any of the settlements, forts, or individual farms, it is uninhabited and for the most part hosts the same trees and other flora as the rest of the Smoke Wood; indeed, botanists consider it part of the Smoke Wood, and it is barely separated from the mainland at all. A half hour's walk from the City, with just a hop, a skip, and a jump across a few stepping stones in the shallow part of the Grande River, and you are there. The island is well worth exploring if you are fond of the woods and wish to experience the beauty of this natural phenomenon. But quiet daytime rambles through the wood are not what Smoke Island is known for.

The Smoke Island Tuck Shop sits at the end of the stepping stone path, providing provisions and trade for those who need to stock up. You can fill up your canteens with water free of charge, or for a silver, proprietress Letitia P. Otter will give you access to the famous Smoke Island Bubble, a shining pool fed by an underground spring behind the shop. It is said that this crystal-clear water is the most refreshing you will ever taste and has healing properties for body and mind. Indeed, some guides will insist on bringing you here to taste the water, which Letitia also sells bottled.

THE WITCH MARKET

During every new moon in spring, summer, and autumn, the Witch Market is active on Smoke Island. The Witch Market is a place to gather and exchange magical ideas and experimentations that may perhaps skirt the edicts in some small way and deviate from the accepted state of normalcy agreed upon by most citizens. The market is a place to trade in prohibited and experimental magical items. It is a black market for weapons, healing agents, oils, plasters, and talismans, but also art, music, and all manner of creative endeavours. The market is a discreet affair, so disguises and concealments are often worn. Fools are not suffered gladly here, so it is best when visiting to stay quiet and respectful; a guide is always helpful in this regard.

Not everyone who attends the Witch Market is completely above-board, nor are they all playing with a full deck, as the sayings go. The Sparrows, it is well known, don't mind the Witch Market and keep a close and subtle eye on things; nothing of significance escapes their notice. Because some of the Witch Market attendees are pushing the bounds of acceptable magical practice and may even be doing a little of their own excavation into Carrion Magics, the Sparrows are keen to learn from these creations and experiences in the hopes that new and unexpected discoveries are made. As you can imagine, some of the more radical Witch Market patrons do not fit neatly into Gwelf society. They have their own ideas and customs and prefer their own company.

Whether you have something to trade or you just want to look around and shop, anyone is welcome. Music, smoke, and drink abound, and the mood is alive with an undercurrent of excitement. It is not necessarily dangerous, although you do need to be cautious; it will take you to the edge of whatever you consider normal and possibly bend your perception of reality. The Witch Market is guaranteed to be an interesting night out.

The market is laid out in an everchanging labyrinth. No two months have the same configuration, geography, merchants, or goods and services for sale. This is what keeps the populace of Gwelf returning again and again, for adventure and discovery. Like the Avenue of Artists, the stalls are not named and see a variety of vendors come and go.

Chapter 10: Landmarks of the City of Gwelf

AFTER YOU HAVE PURCHASED YOUR BOOTS, a sturdy haversack, and enough supplies to keep you well fed and watered on the road, strike out past the main streets to visit some of the incredible landmarks of the City of Gwelf. Remember that while it is generally safe to travel in daylight in the spring and summer, you are always encouraged to hire a guide or guard, or travel in a party.

Badger Hill

Centuries ago, when it became obvious that Ravenkind would wage war on Sparrowkind, the Badgers took it upon themselves to create a safe haven for the citizens of Gwelf. They chose a prominent hill in the area and burrowed in. They made a complex warren of tunnels, hiding places, and traps so baffling that no enemy would ever understand it or find their way through it. Here the people of Gwelf could flee if and when Ravenkind attacked. Since then, the Badgers have added the great amphitheatre Badger Hall, and they have continued to tunnel and build, turning Badger Hill into a proper fortress. The maze of tunnels is yet more sophisticated now, and fortifications have been erected on the perimeter walls, which are watched by the Night Guard.

Badger Hill is the most significant building in Gwelf and considered by many to be the greatest achievement of the Badgers. Not only does it house the largest stage where music and theatre are performed year-round, it is the safest place in the City and gets much use during the autumn and winter months. From a young age, broodlings learn to navigate the intricate tunnel system so they can escape from marauding Ravens, and many families have specific burrows they flee to. Although many sharp clashes have erupted along the Badger Hill defences over the years, no Raven has ever successfully set claw in the Hill.

Badger Hill
in summer

Badger Hill
in winter.

Hildegarde
Sprytail

The Apothecary Garden

Set along the path leading to Badger Hill, the Apothecary Garden
is an enormous green space that was once a flowering meadow. Long ago,
the Sparrows who helped to fortify the City against Ravenkind found that many of the herbs and
flowers they needed for protection and healing grew in harmony in the meadow. They began to tend
the plants more carefully, replacing those they plucked and nourishing particularly successful cultivars.
Little by little, the wild meadow became a garden—still overflowing with natural growth and tending
more toward chaos than order to the untrained eye, but a garden nonetheless. The garden is primarily
tended by Mice in partnership with a few apprentice Sparrows, all under the tutelage of a wise Sparrow
or Mouse on the verge of retirement. Currently, Hildegarde Sprytail Rabbit directs the garden.

Anyone is welcome in the warm and lovely shop at the entrance to the Apothecary Garden.
This fine establishment sells spells and tinctures for just about any ailment. It is the premier spot for
remedies for almost anything of a physical or spiritual nature—though of course, if you're afflicted
with a more supernatural condition, the keepers of the Garden will likely direct you to the Sparrows
of the Sparrow Market or directly to the Archives.

As a tourist, you can pay a copper to wander through the garden, and for two coppers, a guide
Sparrow or Mouse will accompany you and explain what plants are growing, what their uses are,
and how they are best cultivated and harvested. For the botanically minded, this treasure trove
of information is a bargain indeed.

Sparrow Archives

The delicate spires of the Sparrow Archives can be seen from the banks of the Grande River and most vantage points in Gwelf, if you know where to look. Built by the Sparrows and Badgers together in the shape of Smoke Pines, the five towers of the Sparrow Archives rise skyward, but the building also delves seven storeys down, like the roots of the trees it is ensconced within. The Archives house copies of every book and scroll ever written in Gwelf, as well as any texts from outside the territory that the Sparrows can obtain. Scribes work to index and cross-reference this massive collection of knowledge, and the central catalogue is an ever-growing magical list that will send any researcher into a joyous tizzy.

A treasure trove of literary wonders, the Sparrows are very protective of the Archives and have strict rules about their use. There are some texts best left unread, like the famous *Evil Spirits and How to Use Them* by Raven master Riptide. The Sparrows keep these dangerous texts because they see a glimpse into their enemy's mind and magics as a useful tool; to them, there is wisdom in all knowledge.

The archival material itself is held within the large underground portion of the Archives, while the towers are home to much of the action. One of the towers of the Archives is a dwelling for the Sparrow and Mouse historians who work there; it also houses a small library for public viewing. Another of the towers is a scriptorium, one is for practice and experimentation, and the other two hold a university. Students of all creatures are accepted, and the goal of many bright young scholars from across Gwelf is to earn a place of study at the Archives. It is an arduous path, however, and very few are able to withstand the long journey to scholarship. Still, many fine storytellers and local historians who set up shop in pubs across the territory began life as Archives students.

A visit to the Archives is by appointment only, no arms or munitions allowed.

PART III:
VENTURING into the FARMLANDS

Chapter 11: About the Farmlands

FOR MANY, PERHAPS THE MAJORITY, OF VISITORS to the Great Northern Territory, the City of Gwelf is both first and final destination on the itinerary. But we urge even the faintest of heart to consider the Farmlands as a destination. Care is needed, of course, but that is why you have this book—so that you may enjoy the wealth of experiences Gwelf has to offer with a minimum of danger.

The Farmlands go on for miles and miles outside the City of Gwelf, and the best way to explore is on paw. Travellers enjoy going from inn to inn, and you can wander for days, even weeks, this way. Walking is of course the most popular and affordable mode of transportation in Gwelf, so you should have proper, comfortable boots. Bring supplies for your journey and top them up at each inn or farmhouse you pass. While the Farmlands are primarily safe spaces to explore in the summer, you'd best be on your guard. If you have amulets and talismans, wear them; sigils, show them; and if you've ventured into these lands in the autumn or winter, burn your Particle candles to keep Ravenkind at bay.

Three major villages are the hubs of life in the Farmlands, though a number of smaller settlements dot the landscape, and there isn't much of the area that isn't part of someone's farmstead. Redberry Village is the first settlement you will come across if you take the popular Redberry Road out of the City of Gwelf. Following the road northeast will bring you to Applewood Village, which derives its name from the Apple Wood, a wood that is said to have begun life as a Sparrow orchard infused with Earth Magics and left to grow wild for magical research purposes. As thick and wild as any wood, the trees are all fruit bearing, and the village prides itself on its variety of ciders and fruit products. Finally, there is Thistle Village, which rests on the border of the Farmlands and the Scrublands and is mostly protected by Thistle Wood. It is the first village you will come across if you take Thistle Road, the main trade route connecting the Scrublands to the City of Gwelf. Redberry Village and Applewood Village look much like smaller versions of the City of Gwelf, with homes and businesses built into trees and hills. Thistle Village, on the other paw, is much more a product of its proximity to the Scrublands. While it has arboreal structures built into the trees of the protective Thistle Wood, the buildings are also connected by underground tunnels. These are used as pathways at night and in the late autumn and winter. If you visited in the winter and didn't know about the tunnel network, you would think Thistle Village belonged only to the haunts, for you would see no living creature about at all.

List of Equipment

The Farmlands require a slightly different list of equipment than the City; the following is recommended if you are planning a visit to the Farmlands.

- Wet weather gear
- Staff or walking stick, mundane or enchanted
- Camping equipment, including an enchanted tent procured from the Tinkers or requested from your guide
- Arms and armaments to suit your skill, or as your guide prescribes
- Amulets, candles, and talismans
- Other defensive magics: MisMind Traps, Particle ammunition, or grenades, as your guide suggests

Tinkers

✳A Note on Inhabitants: Tinker Bands

There has been only passing mention of the roaming Tinker Bands up to this point, but here in the Farmlands, the Tinkers are more widespread. The Tinkers have no permanent home and travel from campsite to campsite. The bands who travel around the City of Gwelf and the vast tracts of Farmlands and Scrublands are welcomed in Gwelf, as they pose no threat and bring a certain fairground mystique with them wherever they go. There are a few bands who sneak into the Hinterlands and even spend the majority of their time there; these bands, it is rumoured, dabble in Carrion Magics and may even work in dark concert with Ravenkind. Such sinister Tinkers can be distinguished by the perpetual shadows that follow them, no matter the quality of the light around them, the dark bags below their eyes, and their tattered clothing. While these dark Tinkers would not dare to venture as far south as the City of Gwelf or even the Farmlands, they may occasionally be seen in the Scrublands, and you would do well to steer clear of them.

Otherwise, Tinker Bands are quite friendly by all accounts, and true members of the Gwelf citizenry. Should you encounter them on your travels in the Farmlands, you can expect to be received warmly. It is said in the Farmlands that a Tinker camp is equal in comfort and hospitality to any inn or

bed and breakfast. They also have some very effective defensive measures of their own devising, but little is known of these, and they prefer to keep it that way. The Tinkers are made up of a fair mix of creatures that have their own ideas and insist on a free and experimental lifestyle, living in a way quite unlike the other citizens of Gwelf. They tend to form groups or bands and live on the road, outside of the restricted mores of the City and Farmland villages. They stay on the outer fringes of the Farmlands and into the Scrublands, where they have the opportunity to barter and trade with Sparrows, farmers, and adventurers, though they have been known to partake in ransacking and robbing if desperate or frustrated. This is all to say, dear reader, that you should not assume the worst should you encounter the Tinkers. Approach with caution, kindness, and an open mind, and you may just have the best experience of your life among these mysterious and magical creatures. When in doubt, look to your guide.

Chapter 12: Where to Stay in the Farmlands

INN HOPPING IS A VERY POPULAR PASTIME in the Farmlands and may indeed be the reason for your visit to the region. Everyone has their favourite pub or bed and breakfast. Established pub crawl routes are well known and favoured by local revellers. You will find a myriad of inns, bed and breakfasts, rooms for let in opened farmhouses or barns, and campsites in the Farmlands. A room can usually be found on a moment's notice, with the exception of festival seasons, when tourists and citizens from the City of Gwelf flock to the Farmlands. The Autumn Equinox Festival, or Harvest, is a particularly busy time, and a free room is a precious commodity. If you plan to partake of the region's fairs and festivals, it's best to send word ahead and a coin or two to secure a room; accommodations can also be secured through any of the reputable outfitters in the City, or by your guide.

The rivalries between establishments from different areas are very serious. Local Sparrows have been known to step in to give their favourite restaurant or sommelier an extra edge; however, this is not common practice, as Sparrows tend to be somewhat fickle in this matter and have been known to switch allegiances for sport or a particularly rare jar of Smoke Pine honey. But the hope of randomly experiencing an exceptional meal is ever-present and has been known to inspire the occasional pilgrimage (patrons walking for hours or days) as rumours of Sparrow influence flitter through the Farmlands. How grand it would be to have a meal from an establishment with a Sparrow in the kitchen! This is a rare occurrence indeed, as Sparrows have better, more pressing matters to attend to.

The following, then, is by no means an exhaustive list of accommodations and dining establishments in the area. Think of it instead as a starting point for the new traveller. As you wander the pathways of the Farmlands and chat with the creatures you meet along the way, you will certainly learn of other spots that might have only a room or two to let, but also the softest quilt or the spiciest stew or the most calming tea. In turn, recommend your own favourite spots to others you meet and let word spread of the wonders of the Gwelf Farmlands.

Set out with a guide or test the roads on your own. If you're a social type, ask a fellow traveller in the dining room if they'd like to share the road for a time. It's advisable to purchase hard cheese, bread, and other easy-to-carry comestibles before you leave your inn, as well as to fill your canteen, in case a lunch spot doesn't suggest itself as the noon hour approaches. Ask about the specialties of your inn. You might be gifted with preserves, muffins, or a jug of elderberry cordial for your trouble. Nothing is better than a shared bit of cheese, song, cordial, and conversation to accompany you on your path.

Sparrow
Feather Pub

The Pine Cone Inn

Located in Redberry Village, the Pine Cone Inn is a favourite with many travellers. Known for its selection of fine local beers and excellent menu, it's a safe and easy walk for most visitors. With plenty of rooms built into a large Smoke Pine, you will feel warm and secure here. Request a room in the upper trunk for a truly spectacular view of the Farmlands. You can linger for a few days if the fancy takes you. There are plenty of books and a lovely garden in which to read. The dining room is always open, and the beer is cooled in a stream out back.

The Sparrow Feather Pub

A bit farther out in Applewood Village is the Sparrow Feather Pub, which boasts comfortable beds and cozy rooms, making the long trek back to the City unnecessary. After sleeping over in one of their soft feather beds, you'll find a spot waiting for you in the breakfast nook, with a hearty grain-filled, fruit- and yoghurt-topped waffle breakfast and strong, hot tea in the morning.

Mrs. Tuffet's B&B

Tucked away in Thistle Village and owned by the Tuffet Badger clan for at least the last hundred years, a room in Mrs. Tuffet's B&B is a particular treat as you head north. The B&B is built into the side of a hill, with the kitchen and guest rooms near the surface and the Tuffet family living areas deeper underground. Some say Mrs. Tuffet herself has always been the sole proprietress here and estimate her age to be around 150. Boasting four rooms decorated in different themes ("Mushroom Farm," "Badger Hall," "Harvest Time," and "Winter's Sleep"), you may wish to send word and coin ahead to secure a spot. In return, Mrs. T. will share her hearty home cooking, including her storied mushroom soufflé and a glass or three of her famous mushroom moonshine. As she knits, mends, and keeps an eye on the grandbrood (or great-great-grandbrood, depending on who you ask), she'll be more than happy to share a story with you. If you've never experienced the safety and coziness of a night belowground in a Badger burrow, this is a can't-miss experience.

The Tinkers' Meadow

This campground in the eastern Farmlands is a favourite for travellers who want a bit more adventure and perhaps a hint of danger without venturing too far. Though only a few Elder Tinkers stay in this vast, flower-filled meadow, once a year at an undesignated time in the summer season, the Tinker Bands convene. Outsiders are, as a general rule, not welcome at this time. We know that the various groups are said to gather to share stories of their adventures, trade warnings and new scraps of wisdom, barter with one another for goods and services needed, celebrate a few weddings, and exchange youths who, near the cusp of maturity, may want to journey with a different band for a year to learn new perspectives and decide for themselves with whom they wish to make their home.

Watched over by an Elder Tinker or two, the campground is just the right mix of wild and well tended. Buy a defensively charmed tent from the presiding Elders or travel with a guide, who will set you up with anything you might need. You will find the lush meadow a surprisingly soft and comfortable place to rest, and falling asleep with the sound of crickets, the scent of wildflowers, and starshine washing over you is magical in and of itself. In the winter, one might even catch a glimpse of the aurora borealis, though camping out of doors in winter is, of course, not recommended.

Chapter 13: Where to Eat in the Farmlands

Though there may seem to be fewer places for a meal or a pint in the Farmlands than in the City of Gwelf, this is not the case. It is simply that the enjoyment of these establishments must be earned by long walks between them. Everything is more spread out in the Farmlands, so you'll work up a proper hunger and a right hankering for good tea by the time your walk is finished.

As with the accommodations listing, this is only a survey of popular spots you might wish to stop at. We recommend asking fellow travellers and inhabitants of the area. You might find yourself in someone's kitchen, paying for your meal with a song or an afternoon telling stories to the broodlings, or else in a hidden-away pub with three booths and incredible stone fruit pies.

The Ploughman

The first restaurant many encounter after setting off from the Pine Cone for a day's adventure is the Ploughman. Located on Redberry Road between Redberry Village and Applewood Village, this spot is favoured by locals and visitors alike. The Ploughman is an ideal place for a hearty sampling of the region's best seasonal delights. There is no menu here. Simply indicate to the proprietress how hungry you are and you'll find yourself furnished with a small, medium, large, or hungry-farmer-sized wooden tray heaped with nuts, seeds, cheeses, dried and pickled vegetables, mustards, compotes, and anything else the cook could get his clever paws on that morning.

The Sparrow Feather Pub

The Sparrow Feather in Applewood Village gets a second mention here, for not only is it renowned as an inn, it is also a can't-miss spot for a bite to eat. While the proprietors have long been the Kottke Rabbit family, the pub was built in the former home of Turmeric G. Flickertail, a culinary genius of a Sparrow whose kitchen spells are the stuff of legend. The Sparrow Feather is named after this great Sparrow, and some claim that all their recipes came from Turmeric's own cookbook—or grimoire—which is why the food bursts upon your tongue and the memory of the flavours you experience here linger for years.

The Mossy Kettle Pub

This charming pub in Redberry Village is run by the so-called "cousins," a Raccoon named Errol Alderman, who takes care of business matters, and a Rabbit named Huck Rosewood, who supplies the kitchen with delicious produce. Fast friends since they were broodlings, Raccoon and Rabbit are a perfect example of the harmony and opportunity afforded to Gwelf inhabitants when they bring their unique strengths together to create something wonderful. Known for their array of grilled mushrooms, stewed squashes, and crisp carrot and kale salads, the cousins are also the area's premier bakers. Ask for a rhubarb doughnut or a slice of brambleberry pie and be prepared for Errol to paw-deliver it to your table and tell you all about her cousin, who harvested the fruit.

Basil Bushtail

The Witch and Weaver

This Thistle Village pub was founded by Elorina the Fox Witch and her beloved, Basil Bushtail the Weaver. Or so say the Bushtails, who still own the pub today. The story goes that humble Basil, who hailed from the Farmlands, where most of the territory's weavers live, was lost in the woods one night. Stumbling through the towering Smoke Pines until he found himself in the Scrublands, the gentle-spirited Fox came face to face with a group of Mange-stricken creatures. He knew he was done for, but then he saw a strange greenish glow moving through the woods. It was Elorina, surrounded by magical green foxfire. She fought off the Mange-creatures and hurried the terrified Basil to her home to recover from his fright. There, he gave her the gift of his travelling cloak, which he had woven with his own paws. She was so charmed by his fine work that she fell in love with him. They eventually opened their home to other lost travellers, sharing the warmth of Basil's textiles and the potions and spells provided by Elorina to soothe the weary traveller's mind and paws. As you might expect, this pub favours Fox brews, including the fabled Elorina's Foxfire, a green beer that cools the tongue and burns the belly.

The rich textiles that adorn this pub show the artistic flare Foxes are known for, including a never-finished tapestry that runs all around the walls of the dining room. Depicting the family's history, it is taken down and updated each decade by the weavers who still proudly carry on the family business. They leave one edge of tapestry ragged and unfinished, indicating that the story the tapestry tells is not yet done.

Chapter 14: Where to Shop in the Farmlands

THERE IS A DISTINCT DIFFERENCE BETWEEN THE shopping experience in the City of Gwelf and the Farmlands. In the Farmlands, it's not simply about entering a shop, purchasing goods, and heading out once more. Instead, some of the fun is that the shops are part of the larger agricultural operations of the area. Do yourself a favour and don't simply browse and go. Instead, chat with the proprietors and request tours of their operations. Experience the vegetable, fruit, arboreal, apiary, and fungi farms of the Farmlands and gain a greater appreciation for your purchases.

Loambottom Vegetable Stand

A can't-miss stop in the Farmlands is the Loambottom Vegetable Stand, located on Redberry Road between the City of Gwelf and Redberry Village. The Otters sell their produce here and are renowned for their spinach, rice, and edible flowers. You can purchase preserves and beautiful flower infusions to quench your thirst on the road, too. While visiting, request a tour. You've never seen anything like an Otter canal farm. The canals between the raised garden beds act both as freshwater irrigation sources for the plants and provide swimming or boat access between the gardens. For a coin or a story, the Otters will take you by boat to visit the different crops and perhaps even let you harvest a flower or water chestnut for yourself.

Sunlottes Apiary

While shopping for candles at Bailiwick's in the City of Gwelf is recommended, as you should not set out on the road without at least one Particle candle in your pack, you can also stock up at Sunlottes Apiary in the Farmlands. This shop in Applewood Village is home to candles made entirely from the wax of the Sunlotte apiary. The Sunlotte family of Mice are some of the foremost apiarists in the region, and they are renowned for the skill and refinement of their beeswax products.

Many of their products are infused with Particle Magics, and the Particle candles and incense offered at this shop are designed specifically for the various needs of the Farmlands and Scrublands. Particle candles for the home ward off attacks from Ravenkind, and Particle incense for travellers, meant to be burned on the road, offer camouflage. Specialized incense can induce nausea or fear in enemies, while some candles can release a burst of light that dazes lesser dark creatures, causing them to flee to their lairs and await the night. If you have the time and coin, you can even request candles and incense made to your specifications.

There are also, of course, non-magical candles simply for light, heat, and the homey scent of beeswax. You can purchase beeswax statuettes, sealing wax, balms for lips and paw pads, fur treatments, wood polish, and even waxed bookbinding thread. Sunlottes also offers an incredible mead cider of apples and fermented honey. While it doesn't pack much of a punch—unsurprising for a drink meant for a Mouse—this drink uplifts the spirit and fills the drinker with a sunny sense of courage and a warm disposition.

The Fox and Fiddle Tea Shop

Legendary for its local amateur performances, not just by Fox musicians but by anyone who wishes to sing, whistle, play an instrument, or dance a merry jig, this tea shop in Redberry Village is one-third musical venue, one-third tearoom, and one-third shop. Offering over two hundred varieties of wildcrafted teas, you can taste any blend first in the tearoom and then purchase a package to bring home with you.

The Fox and Fiddle is famous for its musk mallow tea, which combines the dried leaves, seeds, and flowers of the musk mallow plant, producing a uniquely nutty tea. Though not to everyone's taste, the astringent thistle and licorice tea is said to be a perfect morning pick-me-up after a night of slightly too much revelry. Our favourite cup is the wild rose blend, which includes the leaves and petals of wild roses and sweet clover and the unopened buds of ox-eye daisies to produce an aromatic cup that is slightly pink and sets the drinker into a pleasant afternoon drowse—perfect for lingering and enjoying whichever musician has taken to the stage.

Raccoon Pick-Your-Own (PYO) Fruits and Berries

Raccoons are clever creatures. They're happy to welcome you onto their land and let you pick your own fruit and pay them for the pleasure of doing so. At the Racoon PYO, in the colloquially known Raccoon Territory of the Farmlands, your entrance fee pays for a woven basket of the finest dried marsh reeds and all the fruit you can fill it with. Additional baskets are of course available for an additional charge—locals can reuse baskets from previous years, and so can you if you are a returning visitor.

While most Raccoon orchards feature towering fruit trees that only expert climbers can scale and tangled berry patches that require sharp eyes and clever paws to secure the sweetest, ripest berries, the PYO is different. It is meant for tourists. The trees are kept at a uniform height, with fruit-laden branches in easy reach of any creature's grasp. The berry fields have even, well-maintained paths that feature bright berries easily identified and plucked. Depending on the time of year, you might walk away with baskets of apples, pears, peaches, brambleberries, blackberries, or barberries. You can also purchase baked goods, fruit preserves, syrups, and cordials from the small shop at the entrance where you pay for admission and baskets.

Chapter 15: Landmarks of the Farmlands

THE FARMLANDS THEMSELVES ARE SOMETHING OF A landmark within Gwelf. We cannot recommend enough that you hire a guide and let yourself wander the lush countryside, pausing to nap beneath an ancient oak, pick flowers or berries along the roadside, or discover a lost path untravelled for decades. The farmers of the region are famous for their hospitality, outstanding even among the very friendly Gwelf citizenry, and you will be in for a treat every time you call out a greeting to a farmer in a field or knock on the door of a farmstead. Among the farms, rolling hills, and clustered woods, there are some notable things to see in the Farmlands during the spring and summer months. A short list of these follows.

The Floating Bridge at Albion Falls

Albion Falls, just outside Thistle Village, has always been considered a magical, even sacred, spot in the Farmlands, with multiple branches of the cataract tumbling through roots of ancient Smoke Pines. The crystal-clear pools at the base of the falls are a favourite swimming spot, as the water here is naturally warmed by the thermogenic Smoke Pines (bring swimwear!). It is said that the water of Albion Falls is the purest, cleanest water in all of Gwelf and has healing properties to soothe weary bodies and souls. The banks of the river make for fine picnicking.

Before the bridge was built, rafts were used to ford the Albion, which one must cross in order to get to and from either the Scrublands or the region to the south where the City and surrounding areas lie. As this route is essential for trade, it was eventually decided to build a bridge. The easiest route would have been to build across a calm part of the river, but the Sparrows decided to harness the natural warmth of the Smoke Pines in order to keep the bridge free of snow and ice and therefore safe for travel all year-round. Thus, the Floating Bridge, a marvel of Badger, Otter, and Sparrow joint engineering, was built.

Market at Blossomtime

Cherry Hill Gate and the Roadside Market

The Cherry Hill Gate is a funny sort of ouroboros of a landmark. No one is sure which came first: the gate or the Roadside Market that calls the hill home. But of course, Cherry Hill itself predates the rest. It receives its name from the cherry trees that flourish on and around it. In the spring, the hill becomes a glorious blanket of delicate pink blossoms. For the botanically minded, there is no finer experience than taking in the blossoms in spring. You would do well to book your room and guide ahead of time if you would like to visit during Blossomtime. The trees here produce multiple rounds of blooms, and as each new flowering wilts, its petals drop from the tree, and a new bud of a deeper shade of pink takes its place. The Cherry Hill blossoms begin almost white, and after five or six rounds of blossoms from spring to summer, they darken into a scarlet shade the colour of the cherries themselves. As the petals fall, artisans gather them to make a variety of products, which are available for sale at the Roadside Market.

Long ago, some concerns were expressed by the Rabbits of the region that travellers from within and without the territory were taking advantage of the hill's bounty, plucking blossoms before they had fully flowered, overharvesting the trees, and trampling the fertile ground. With the help of the

Sparrows, an enchanted fence inscribed with protection runes and other magical deterrents was erected around the hill. Though not tall, the fence prevents any from climbing over, tunnelling under, or flying above. Instead, access to the hill can only be attained through the Cherry Hill Gate, which is tended to by the Rabbits of the area, who act as stewards of the hill and its bounty.

The Roadside Market by the hill is a notable point of interest in Gwelf, and a useful place to stop if you are bound for adventure beyond the Farmlands. As you might imagine, much of what is sold here includes ingredients from the cherry trees. Here is just a sampling of what you might find: cherry blossom teas, potpourris, and incenses; cherry fur and feather dyes (very popular for use during festivals); cherry pies, scones, and tarts; cherry spreads, relishes, and preserves; cherry juices, wines, and cordials; and cherry ointments and tinctures for arthritis and gout. Weavers and clothiers often set up shop at the Roadside Market as well, selling their fine flax threads and cloths dyed a range of pinks and reds with—you guessed it—cherries! Menders will fix the holes in your clothes and haversack for a small fee. Cobblers will mend your boots or provide you with a brand-new pair for a very reasonable price. You will also find the usual assortment of chandlers selling Particle candles to aid your journey, smiths with tables of daggers and knives, fletchers to refill your quiver and restring your bow, and Mice who have brought magical herbs and enchantments from their Sparrow counterparts to help travellers on the road.

Market at Blossomtime

PART IV:
THE SURVIVAL GUIDE:
SCRUBLANDS and HINTERLANDS

Chapter 16: Preparing for Survival in the Scrublands

ALTHOUGH THE FARMLANDS GO ON IN ALL directions for many miles, they eventually come to an end. The wise traveller will not pass beyond this region if they wish to stay safe and enjoy the journey home with a heart full of joyous adventure and tales of their time in Gwelf.

There are some, however, who will insist on adventuring farther, leaving the idyllic beauty of the Farmlands and the City of Gwelf behind. If you are stout of heart, well prepared with knowledge, arms, and Defensive Magics, and have a trusty guide beside you, a trip into the Scrublands will provide you with the excitement you are looking for. Upon entering this area of the territory, you will find yourself in a much different environment. The Scrublands are a wild and dangerous country that shields the peaceful Farmlands from the Hinterlands beyond the border. This is the frontier where the war between Ravenkind and Sparrowkind is primarily waged. Beyond that, into the Hinterlands themselves. This journey will require serious preparation and is not recommended for most travellers.

A Note on Defensive Magics and Equipment

It is not enough to be well armed, though being able to go on the offence is, of course, absolutely necessary in this dangerous region. You must invest in multiple protections for yourself. With any luck, you will pass unheeded by the wretched inhabitants here, but this is likely not going to be the case, so preparation is paramount.

Have your gear inscribed with sigils before you venture out, wear at least one amulet around your neck, have a pocket full of talismans, and obtain a glyph in the City or at the Witch Market. Be sure to request it be inscribed somewhere visible—Home Guard often ask to see glyphs, sigils, amulets, and talismans as a matter of course if they meet you on the road beyond the Farmlands, else they may turn you back or direct you to the nearest Sparrow or mage. This is to protect the unwary traveller who might wander accidentally into the Scrublands and find themselves at the merciless claws of Ragteeth, Rats, and Ravens.

As you look for the right combination of magics to protect you, think about your strengths and weaknesses. Be brutally honest with yourself. Discuss these with your guide. For example, you might require a talisman to ward against clumsiness, a glyph to enhance a keen sense of hearing, and a sigil to protect from complacency. You might have your weapons outfitted with sigils to improve aim, increase the might of a blow, or make you appear to be more fearsome in the eyes of the enemy. Finally, procure as many Particle candles and products as possible to keep foul creatures at bay.

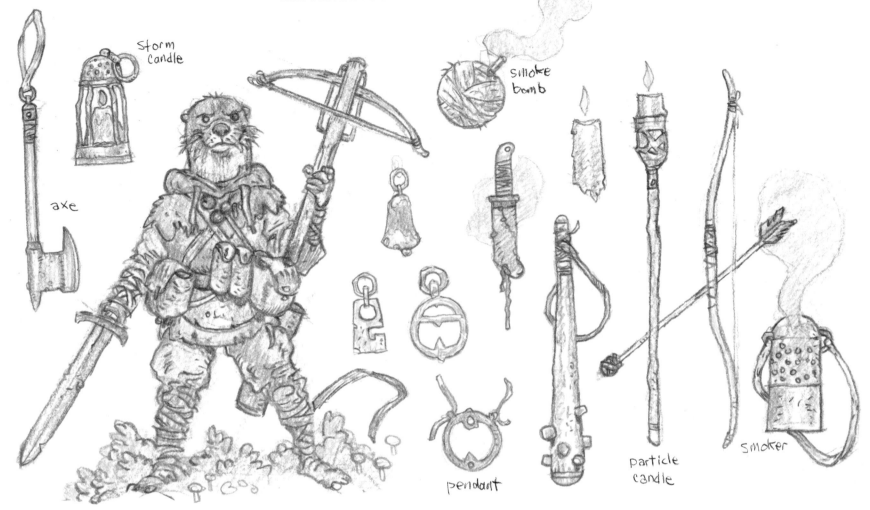

storm candle

smoke bomb

axe

pendant

particle candle

smoker

List of Equipment

It is here that the somewhat cheeky title of this book becomes less playful. This book truly is your survival guide now. Read carefully, stock up on the items below in the City of Gwelf (see pages 60 to 72), the Witch Market (see page 75), and the Roadside Market (see pages 104 and 105) before you dare set paw on the road out of the Farmlands.

— Tinker- or Sparrow-inscribed camping gear
— Haversack, boots, canteen, and rations
  (hardtack, seed cheese, saltfish, dehydrated vegetable leather, medicinal whisky)
— Long-burning Particle candles
— Amulets and talismans as necessary
— Particle-imbued arms and armaments as suit your skill, or as your guide prescribes
— MisMind, Stonk, and/or other Particle-infused projectiles and traps
— Health poultices, potions, and tinctures, else hire or befriend a healer mage

Chapter 17: When to Visit the Scrublands

Don't.

Oh, very well, if you want more in-depth advice than that, we can only plead with you to make your journey in the summer, when Ravenkind activity is always naturally at its lowest, the sun is warmest, and the fog is thinnest. Second safest is spring, though because so little grows here, there is not much to recommend the season. You will find yourself caught in slick, icy muds and alternating flurries and flash floods, so while there might not be as much Raven activity, nature itself might be the cause of your downfall.

We cannot urge you strongly enough to avoid the autumn and winter in this unforgiving land. There is no good reason to visit at this time. Only those on business, with the Home Guard, looking for an intense and deadly journey, with poor timing, or who lose themselves along the twisting pathways will wander here. Few who venture to the Hinterlands make it back alive in these cold seasons.

Guides of the Scrublands and Beyond

We have never heard tell of a visitor to the territory, no matter how brave, no matter how battle-hardened, who returned from a solitary journey into the Hinterlands. Nothing will prepare you well enough, not even this survival guide. You need a sure-pawed outfitter to see you through, a creature who will ensure you have the kit and weaponry required, who will take you to the Sparrows for the heaviest Defensive Magics, who will show you the way through the tangled paths of the Scrublands and beyond.

Most guides are retired Home Guards. Some miss the thrill of the hunt; others feel they can still be of service on the frontier and use travellers as a means to pay their way back out to the Hinterlands to uncover routes into the Boreals and Ravenkind secrets. Exceptional guides don't come cheap. If you must test your mettle in this area of Gwelf, spare your coins (and your life) and hire the best.

We also recommend that, depending on your own experience, you hire an extra guard or guide, as well as a mage of any sort and an exorcist to join your party. While hauntings in the Farmlands and southern areas of the territory are charming at best and irritating at worst, the ghosts of the Scrublands, Border Region, and Hinterlands are a different kettle of chestnuts. At best, they will make you cold and draw your concentration from your task; at medium they will draw the Ravens' or Mange-creatures' attentions to you; and at worst they will possess you, so hungry and desperate for warmth and life that they will attempt to find it within your body. A mage will help misdirect and fend off these creatures, while an exorcist will renew your charms and Defensive Magics and drive back more persistent haunts.

Chapter 18: The Dark Creatures of the Scrublands and Border Region

WHILE YOU MAY FEEL YOU HAVE GOTTEN to know the kinds of inhabitants you will encounter in the territory in the previous chapters of this book, we now introduce you to a range of nightmare beings from beyond the border. If you are lucky, you will never encounter one in your lifetime. If you are unlucky, you will face one, but with courage, preparation, and strong defences, live to tell the tale. And if you are the sort to seek out adventure at any cost...well, perhaps we will meet one day at the Mossy Kettle and you can recount the tale of how you managed to return in one piece.

Ravens, Rats, and Ragteeth

While the Ravens do not actually live in the Scrublands or Border Region, you must still be aware of their presence and influence here. The creeping blight that saps the land of its fertility, the appearance of Mange-creatures, the nests of Ragteeth and Rats all stem from the threat of Ravenkind.

Stay vigilant. The Ravens are always probing along the border, looking for weaknesses. They launch random harassments to keep the Guards off balance while searching for better routes in and out of Gwelf. The Ravens use what we have come to call "machinations" in their tactics. The Ravens themselves generally sit in flying devices that look like chairs from which they can drop Carrion bombs, Mange spores, or even invading Ragteeth and Rats. The Ravens, we think, are primarily interested in three things: claiming victims, disrupting the peace in Gwelf, and obtaining as much Particle Magics as possible.

Rats are the smallest and most numerous of the Ravenkind forces we face. They are stealthy and move around unseen, breaking and entering, setting fires, poisoning wells with Mange, stealing items imbued with Particle Magics, and snatching what bodies (live or otherwise) they can for their Raven masters. Rats like to stay in the shadows and prefer to leave unseen. They have nests scattered throughout the Scrublands and Border Region, with more still living in the Muskeg and among the Frost Pines of the Boreal Mountains. We can only imagine that the Hinterlands are infested with these wicked creatures.

Once upon at time, Ragteeth were things unknown in Gwelf, but alas, they press past the Border more and more often. They are not endemic to the southern part of the Territory, and no one knows much about their anatomy, psychology, or society. If one were to hazard a guess you might say a Ragtooth, sometimes referred to as a swarmer, is a transmuted creature, a mixture of both Rat and Raven. It is suspected that the Ravens created them with their Carrion Magics and set them loose in Gwelf where they can to sow terror and confusion. They flock or swarm like Rats and they attack without mercy until stopped. They eat everything, break everything, and kill everything. There are specialized hunting teams that patrol the Scrublands and the Border Region for roving swarms of Ragteeth, intent on stopping them in their tracks. Often knife and sword are the only way to deal with this menace, as the dark Raven magics from whence these creatures are borne are constantly changing and are difficult to combat with any

consistent Particle magic. These creatures are exactly why camping is not recommended in the Scrublands. If you insist on camping here be sure to post guards, light all your storm candles and have Particle grenades to hand. If you encounter these creatures you will be in a fight for your life. Evasion is the best tactic.

A Raven attack will usually involve a diversion and a primary strike. The diversion will come in the form of an incursion by Mange-creatures driven by Rats or Ragteeth. The strike will be an aerial attack by Ravens in flight-chairs casting spells and dropping traps, then stealing victims from the ground and flying off with them back to the Boreal Mountains, trailed and guarded by the returning Rats or Ragteeth. If the Ravens don't find a body, they will often resort to vandalism and arson to draw the good creatures of Gwelf out where any lone citizen might easily be captured. So be wary; Ravenkind are devious.

116

Mange

The Ravens are quite adept at toxins and plagues, this being the outcome of centuries of Carrion study. This is one of their advantages, and with it they have created the Mange. Mange, as we understand it, is a disease of Raven machination and spreads as an average contagion, or else through well poisonings or targeted Mange drops. Mange-creatures, at the beginning, were primarily Rats set loose at the border and pointed in the direction of the City of Gwelf. Today, sadly, many a Mange-creature is simply an ordinary, innocent Gwelf citizen infected by the disease. These creatures do not use sword or bow, bite or rend, plan or trap; they simply grab onto the next victim of Mange and hold tight like a clinging vine. They will never let go. If the Mange-creature is not somehow removed, then the afflicted creature and their victim will eventually starve together and die. Particle candles (when lit) will prevent the Mange-creatures from finding you, so be sure to have a good supply when travelling in the Scrublands and beyond. If they do find you, then you will want to use Stonk or Particle grenade, which will be very effective. If the Mange-creature has been infected for only a day or two, a good dose of Particle healing may rescue them from the contagion, and, though they might be missing an appendage, they could yet survive and return to normal life. Usually, however, the victim is never found by those who are looking for them.

Floaters and Walking Wood Demons

Floaters are the size of a bucket and filled with scrap wood or bone, rope, and rags, then doused with skunk oil and the Mange virus, lit on fire, and set adrift aerially, on the breeze aboard a flight-chair, or else aquatically on a waterway. The Ravens release and allow Floaters to drift over the border, where they can land randomly throughout the region. If a Floater goes off in a public place, it is considered a Mange bomb, but if it comes down in the wild somewhere, it is considered a booby trap that has splashed its toxic soil a radius of fifty paces or so and is just waiting for an unwitting soul to wander through it and spread the Mange even further. Wild and domestic animals are just as susceptible to it as citizens. Nothing will ever grow again where one of these things has come down and gone off. It's the most toxic thing known to Gwelf.

More recently (as of this writing), a variation, or abomination, of this weapon has been sighted
in the Hinterlands. The Guard call them the Walking Wood Demons. These machinations are the much
larger and more dangerous version of their Floater cousins. The Wood Demons shamble across country,
set on fire and pointed towards the border, where they will stagger in among the Home Guards and
explode. The Wood Demon explosions are much larger than Floater blasts and have a much wider effective
radius, sowing more fear and lethality than ever before. It is not uncommon for border units to quail at the
site of an approaching Wood Demon and flee their positions.

You will smell a Wood Demon long before you see it. Your guide will know the protocol, but if
you are alone, the most important thing to do is hightail it to the nearest Home Guard post and alert them.

Chapter 19: Overview of the Scrublands

THE SCRUBLANDS ARE A WILDER AND MORE dangerous country than the Farmlands. This area provides a sort of bulwark between the peaceful Farmlands and the border where the war between the Ravens and the Sparrows rages. This journey will require serious preparation and is not recommended.

But we must assume that if you have read this far, it is because you truly wish to see this stark but beautiful country for yourself. And it is our job to prepare you. Take heed, adventurer. There are no shortcuts to be foolishly attempted here. The only way you will survive is through preparation, training, and the skill of your guide and fellow party members.

The Scrublands gets its name from the terrain and plant life, or lack thereof, that characterize it. While not a dead land, life certainly has to fight to take hold here. Two major Sparrow-protected woods grow here, from which the locals collect firewood, building supplies, and a variety of foraged foods such as mushrooms, grasses, and berries. Otherwise, the land is covered by bare rock, lichen, groundcover plants, and scrubby prairie grass. Apart from a brief flourishing of green leaves and a rainbow of tiny buds in high summer, the land is generally a wash of browns and beiges. To the visiting eye, it might seem

Badger Fairy mushroom, can be eaten raw, cooked, or dried.

quite uniform and even boring; but Scrublanders focus on the myriad textures and hues within their landscape and capture the land in a gorgeous variety of art. They are especially known for their quilts and other textiles, as well as their heavily textured, almost three-dimensional oil paintings. The style of Badger art here is called claw painting, in which the artist uses their claws to cake, shape, and carve thick oil paints on their canvases.

The cuisine here is markedly different from that in southern Gwelf. While the bounty of the Farmlands is accessible by major trade roads, the journey is made less frequently in both directions. Scrublanders stay safe within their villages as much as possible, and farmers and peddlers don't venture north from the Farmlands much. The Gwelf Council sponsors several trade fairs throughout the year, sometimes employing willing Tinker Bands or guides who are between jobs to lead caravans of merchant goods to the Scrublands, always under the protection of the Home Guard. Otherwise, the Scrublanders make do with what they can coax from their land. Mushrooms, berries, pine needle tea, various saps and syrups tapped from the woods, lichens, and particularly protein-rich roots and tubers make up the bulk of the Scrublander diet, along with long-lived root vegetables, preserves, and honeys from the caravans. The Scrublanders like it this way. They are hardy creatures who take pride in their close relationship with the land, and most say they have no interest in moving south, where they scoff at the easy and less rewarding lives they see there.

As with the rest of Gwelf, all the populations are represented in this area, but there is a great concentration of Sparrows and Mice here, as well as Badgers and Rabbits. With smaller tributaries forking their way through this land, you'll find fewer Otters, and the Foxes and Raccoons of Gwelf tend to prefer the more urban areas to the south where they can ply their trades, but a few hardy families and magically inclined apprentices from these groups call the Scrublands their home.

Dundurn Village

Though you will find several tiny settlements scattered across the Scrublands, Dundurn Village is the only major settlement in the area, named after the mighty Badger who founded the village in the tunnels. Dundurn is carved into the very land and has no tree cover. The architectural style is much different from anywhere else in Gwelf, as none of its structures are built into trees or hillsides. Instead, half-storey rock dwellings are dug into the earth and heavily protected by runes, and the village itself spreads out in tunnels belowground. While Thistle Village's tunnels are used as pathways between their more traditionally arboreal structures (see page 86), Dundurn's entire village exists in the tunnels, with homes and businesses built into large, fortified burrows. As such, none of the Scrubland Sparrows live in the village, preferring aboveground or treetop dwellings and visiting only on business. Dundurn Village is the closest settlement to the main Border Fort (see pages 139 and 140), and it is where most of the northern Home Guard live when they are not on duty.

Chapter 20: Where to Stay in the Scrublands

THE FIRST THING TO KNOW IS THAT when staying in Dundurn Village, you will be staying belowground. We've known a few fine adventurers who discover their own claustrophobia and must take their leave of the village prematurely. While the network of tunnels between the subterranean buildings is well lit, you'd nonetheless be wise to have Particle candles at paw, as well as a talisman of finding, which will allow a search party to locate you quickly if you become lost.

There is only one inn in the Scrublands, but there are a few boarding houses and rooms to let in each small town, and should your case be dire, requests can be made with the Sparrows or at a nearby Border Fort. Remember, no matter how haunted your shelter, it can still be a safe place to stay if the occupying spirits are not too dangerous or moody, and all safety precautions followed. And of the many enemies to fear, haunts should be the least of your party's worries.

Dundurn Village Inn

Dundurn Village, as the only true settlement in the Scrublands, is naturally home to its only proper inn, numbering ten beds. The owners, Peter and Porter van Sickle, are famous for debating whether to board some of the rooms up or add more rooms on, depending on the season, the number of tenants they have, and how many have not returned from their adventures. Porter, who takes care of the cooking for the inn, believes the tourist trade has increased over the past decade and argues for an increase in rooms, while Peter, who keeps the rooms, books, and records, has a tally of those who have not returned and believes customers are on the decline.

While not, perhaps, as luxurious as the Belle Flower in Gwelf City, Dundurn Village Inn is nonetheless not lacking for convenience and comfort. While we cannot speak for the view it offers, as it's underground, it is located centrally within the village, and with the help of a guide or a map, you will be able to find your way to any of the shops you might wish to patronize. The pawspun Pony-hair blankets and famous Sparrow-feather bedticks guarantee you will feel cozy and well rested. The Sparrow feathers offer protection from nightmares, and this is why adventurers who have seen the horrors of the enemy prefer to sleep here, allowing their minds to decompress and let go of fear before continuing homeward. At any given time, you will find fellow adventurers, seekers of Sparrow lore, brave peddlers, and the kin of posted Home Guards staying at the inn. At certain times of year, you will also find traders from the southern areas of Gwelf who have brought preserves, medicines, cloth, and weaponry. Generally, trade caravans go to Dundurn in spring and early autumn, ensuring the villagers, other Scrublands inhabitants, and Home Guard have access to what goods they will need throughout the year.

Camping in the Scrublands

When you overnight outside the relative safety of the village, you must be prepared to camouflage and defend your camp. This experience is nothing like camping in the Farmlands. You must be wily, fearless, and perhaps a little lucky. Camping is always an option, and sometimes the only one, but it comes with its own set of unique challenges. Securing your site and establishing a perimeter is of paramount importance. You will have to be armed with the appropriate weapons and Defensive Magics. A proximity bell will let you know if anything gets inside your perimeter. Long-burning Particle candles and torches will keep the smouldering Particle Magics in the air, deterring most

Long burning particle candle

iron sparrow pendant

interlopers. Be sure to always have someone on guard, and everyone must have on their talismans with sigils properly displayed. If you are travelling with a guide, they will likely be armed with a longbow and possibly a sword or edged weapon for defence. You may also want to consider a personal weapon if you have skill or your guide or group leader feels it is necessary. A knife, cudgel, sword, or staff are good for paw-to-paw fighting, if it should happen to come to that. A longbow or crossbow are good for long-range defence. Follow the advice of your guide and be ready to move quickly—there are no second chances in the Scrublands.

Chapter 21: Where to Eat in the Scrublands

ANY SCRUBLANDER WE INTERVIEWED FOR THIS SECTION scoffed when asked about "dining" options. To the Scrublanders, food is merely a means to an end: a full belly means an easy rest means a sharp mind and a quick paw, that's it. This serves as a reminder that you should most certainly stock up on provisions before exiting the Farmlands. Bring food that takes up little room but is long-lasting, such as crusty bread, seed cheese, dried berries, teas, and dehydrated vegetable stews that can be cooked in your tin kettle over a fire.

Your Inn or Resting Place

Rather than retreading ground, we shall simply say here that the Dundurn Village Inn, any boarding house, and any household with a room to let will provide you with a meal as part of your room rate. Indeed, any place offering accommodation will likely open their kitchen to you for a price. Most Scrubland accommodations do not have a proper dining room, let alone menu, however, so your options are the proverbial "take it or leave it." We recommend that you take it.

Most proprietors are interested in coin or story; depending on the time of year, they may also wish for certain hard-to-find ingredients or goods from other areas of Gwelf. A guide worth their salt will know what to bring to trade with innkeepers. Particle candles, amulets, talismans with interesting or unusual effects, bottled water from the Smoke Island Bubble, toys from the City, and honey from Sunlottes Apiary are excellent choices.

Dundurn Hill Market

As mentioned, Dundurn Village is an almost entirely subterranean settlement. On its eastern border lies a hill, one of the few in the flat Scrublands. Ages ago, Sparrows and Badgers worked together to hollow out the hill, creating a spacious marketplace. Vendors of all kinds set up shop here.

Foraging in the Scrublands

This is not recommended if you do not know what you are doing. Many of the grasses and weeds here are poisonous, or at the least, non-nutritive. You do not wish to fill up on what you think is a nutritious grass only to discover you've bloated yourself on something that will pass through you without giving you energy. Guidebooks like *The Herbs and Edibles of Gwelf: A Forager's Guide* by Millicent Lorenza Mouse, available at Root Cellar Books, is a great choice, but a copy or two should be obtainable in the Dundurn Hill Market. Your guide should also be well versed in foraging in the Scrublands. Forageables here include lichens and mosses, mushrooms, whip grass, snow lilies, and false smoke roots.

Requesting Sparrow Hospitality

A Sparrow will never say no to a fellow creature in need. Indeed, Sparrows are even known to give hospitality to injured Rats on the run from the Ravens. They often aid Tinkers separated from their bands, or adventurers who've taken the wrong trail. While hoping to stumble upon a hidden and defensively warded Sparrow cottage in the Scrublands should not be your only plan, a Sparrow will always welcome you into their home if you come across them, or better yet, if they discover you. It is a great honour to be in a Sparrow's home. Speak only when spoken to. Do not ask impertinent questions. Do not try to show off. Do not request the Sparrow perform magics for you, especially not for your entertainment. But do graciously accept any offer of help, magical or mundane. Do accept any lessons, stories, or history the Sparrow wishes to share with you. Listen well and commit what you hear to memory. In return, offer a story of your own. Sparrows rarely wish for material items, but most will accept an anecdote from your life, a lesson you have learned elsewhere, help with some small jobs in their homes, a song, or even a joke as thanks for aid.

Chapter 22: Places to Avoid in the Scrublands

THE SCRUBLANDS ARE A VAST AREA FULL of danger. Do not be fooled by the map, which might make it seem like an empty land. A journey here will always include risk, be it from the elements or enemies. Here are a few sites you should know about as you embark.

The Cursed Battlefield at Raventag

If you are considering visiting Raventag, an activity we in good conscience cannot sanction, you must realize that this site is haunted by forces that no exorcist can contain. The ancient battlefield has become a destination for adventure tourists craving a dark and edgy experience. The effects of being in this place vary greatly; it is devoid of all life force: there is no sound, no scent, and no wind, just an oppressive void. Spells will not work normally here, and many visitors feel the weight of the horror and flee.

No creature fully understands the effect of the Sparrow weapon that devastated the battlefield that day and how the Earth Magics might have interacted with the Raven's own Carrion Magics. The fallout was toxic, and the outcome so unprecedented that no elder on either side can explain or undo it. If you have a choice, do not go to this place of evil.

Graveyard on Cluster Hill

Many of the casualties from the Raventag catastrophe who eventually succumbed to their injuries were buried here and never found peace. They continue to haunt the area as full-fledged ghosts, seeking revenge on Raven and Sparrowkind alike. This in many ways could actually be the most dangerous site in the entire region. While of course the dead had to be honoured and put to rest after Raventag, it was perhaps an ill-fated decision to place a graveyard so close to the border. The creep of Carrion corruption has infiltrated the very soil here, leaving the spirits restless and entirely unexorcisable. Reports of moving headstones and night screams are well documented and should be taken seriously. Many an exorcist has tried to lay these poor, tortured souls to rest, but none has been successful. For the ghost-hunting adventurer, this is the most prized place to visit. However, disappearances are common, and whole groups have been known to go missing. Please heed this warning and resist the temptation to visit Cluster Hill. Only sorrow and pain await you there. These ghosts are more restless and more dangerous than others in Gwelf. Beware.

Chapter 23:
Overview of the Hinterlands

THE FARTHER YOU PLUNGE INTO THE SCRUBLANDS, the closer you will come to the border that separates the Region of Gwelf from the Hinterlands—in other words, the domain of Ravenkind. This means watchtowers and outposts will become common sights along the roads, and you will begin to encounter Home Guard defence units (mounted and on paw) on a fairly regular basis. They are heavily armed and carry dangerous Particle weapons that require training and experience to manage.

No villages or other settlements exist in the Border Region or in the Hinterlands. There are no plucky families tending hard-won farms or skillful foragers eking out a living here. Instead, you will find the mighty trees of the Border Wood, several heavily defended forts, and a stretch of Muskeg that separates Gwelf from the foothills of the Hinterlands and Boreal Mountains.

The border is not so finite as the map makes it look: it goes on for many, many miles in both directions, zigging and zagging where land is won, lost, or unclaimed. There are no safe places here, not even in summer. Beyond the border, the grim tundra stretches out for days, watched over by forts and fortified positions of both Sparrow- and Ravenkind. You must remember that you are now in the middle of a supernatural battlefield. The tundra breathes and moans. The wind howls and burns with toxins and smoke. Every shadow moves of its own accord.

In all honesty, if you have managed to get this far, there is little we can do to help you, and you should rely on your own skill and experience as well as that of your guide and any compatriots you travel with. In the pursuit of writing this book, we, the Council, sent Wilburton Fox to travel with a heavily armed guide and patrol group, risking life and appendage to discover just what draws creatures to this terrifying area. There are several reasons that he reported: first, the sense of danger. For some, being tucked up in bed with a good book and a good cup of tea is truly the height of a vacation well spent and indeed even a life well lived. This is the life for our dear Wilburton. But for others, life is not truly life without the hint of danger, the possibility of terror, harm, and death faced and evaded. And it's these folks who find themselves in the Border Region, actively seeking fights with Ragteeth, Rats, and Ravens.

Ravens

Ragtooth

Rats

A second, more convincing, reason is scholarship. Like those who thirst for danger, there are brilliant minds who thirst for knowledge, and for whom knowledge already learned and recorded in a book by some other scholar is not enough. Scholars of history, botany, geology, sociology, and of course magics, as well as many an artist and author who hope to be inspired, plan expeditions to the Hinterlands every year. And, might we add, every year fewer than half those parties return with their numbers intact. We owe a great debt to these scholars and artists, though. It is through them that we know as much as we do about the lands beyond the Scrublands.

Third, and finally, there is the draw of magics. Please don't take this as encouragement, but many adventurers and Home Guards who have spent time in the Hinterlands say that the magics here are stronger than any they've ever felt. It makes sense, for here is the battleground of Earth and Carrion Magics, of Sparrow- and Ravenkind fighting for dominance. The ground is steeped in their spellwork and experiments. It is showered with Particle Magics from Stonk, grenade, and arrow. It is salted with the corpses of Ravenkind's felled abominations, their demons and plague carriers, taken down by Sparrows and the Home Guard. Strange things happen here. Plants that have never been seen anywhere else thrive here. It is a fascinating place to practice the magical arts, and that draw might be intoxicating.

The Threat of the Hinterlands

Threats here are innumerable: from the creeping tundra to the uncharted Muskeg, from the roving Rat bands to the Walking Wood Demons, you cannot imagine the many dangers here. Expand your imagination, then, and consider the unimaginable. So few Gwelf citizens or adventurers have ventured beyond the border and returned that next to nothing is known of the Hinterlands and the great Boreal Mountains. If you do venture out there, and if you do return, please tell us of your adventures.

✳ A Note on the Tinker Bands in the Hinterlands

What happens in the Hinterlands on a dark winter night is anyone's guess. Are the Tinkers making pacts with the Ravens? Are they delving into the unknowns of Steam Consciousness with the Ravens, seeking out ancestors and powers untapped by Sparrows? Spies and Sparrows presume as much, but they also predict that these Tinkers are wading into a relationship that is over their ears. Whatever the secrets there, we suggest that if you should happen to come across a Tinker camp in the Hinterlands, give it a wide berth. They are likely to present themselves as peaceful, happy wanderers, which they in fact may be, but here it is far more likely that you will find a knife at your throat and a claw in your pocket. Your guide will know best what course of action to follow; trust them.

Flying
Raven
Chairs.

snippers

stabber

tooth puller

axe

Weaponry of the Ravens

We have already discussed the many minions of the Ravens: Rats, Ragteeth, Mange-creatures, and their mechanized weapons the Floaters and Walking Wood Demons (see page 118 and 119). But it is here in the Border Region and Hinterlands where you will likely encounter an actual Raven mage, generally flying about on a mechanized flight-chair, or else being carried around in a palanquin by a band of Rats. Be aware: a Raven is rarely surprised, and if you encounter one, it is perhaps at their behest and not yours. The Home Guard reports that they carry with them long hooks for ensnaring victims while in flight. They fly low over the treetops to avoid detection, so always keep an eye out, especially at dusk. Powerful, long-burning Particle candles will keep them from accidentally discovering you, but if they are tracking you, then direct magical confrontation is your only option.

Little is known to the general citizenry of Carrion Magics, but be aware that their spells are nothing like the protections and Particle Magics of the civilized Gwelf. Instead you will see spells that poison, disease, or otherwise inflict their victim; there may be spells that steal one's life force, draw one's energy, or simply maim a creature. Finally, the Ravens reportedly have a certain amount of control over the land, particularly on the tundra. If you venture there, be prepared with as much warmth spells and sigils as you can muster.

gruesome fork.

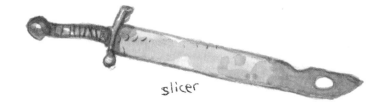

slicer

snatcher hook

Stonk and Petard

Stonk!

Anti-Raven Particle Magics

The new Raven weapons have naturally spurred the Sparrows to keep up with, and hopefully overtake, their relentless foe. To counteract the Floaters and Wood Demons, the Sparrows have come up with something new, which they call a "Stonk." A Stonk is essentially a wooden tube weapon fired from the shoulder that launches a Particle projectile towards its target. These are highly advanced weapons for the Sparrows and have an effective range of four hundred paces. The projectiles are fitted with proximity fuses and explode when near rather than on their target. The explosion is an impressive starburst of glittering smoke and expanding clouds of Particle Magics. With the proper mixture, one Stonk missile will bring down a Floater or stop a Wood Demon in its tracks. The Stonk are now being tried against Rats and Ragteeth; however, demand is far greater than supply. Experiments are currently underway to develop a Stonk that will bring down a Raven, but so far mixed results are the best that can be achieved.

Chapter 24: Surviving and Exploring in the Hinterlands

It is here, dear reader, that we cannot give you detailed geographical insights or describe architecture, favourite meals, beloved folk heroes, and seasonal festivities. There are no inns or interesting foodstuffs to forage; there are no delightful shops to enhance your journey or in which to find souvenirs. It is simply wilderness, and what you encounter there may be Sparrow or Ravenkind, so stay alert, stay safe, and keep within eyesight of your travel companions.

Camping in the Hinterlands

Without inns, you must make do with camping.

First, it is important to have an enchanted camouflage tent paired with your own talismans and amulets. Talismans of warding will act with the camouflage spell to ensure that no matter the land where you are making camp, your tent will blend in. You should have the smallest tent possible: enough room for yourself, your weapons, and your haversack, and no more. It should be low to the ground—not something you can stand up in. This will make it stand out less as Ravens do their nightly sweeps, their hooks in their claws as they search for new victims.

Second, while we recommend bringing flint and steel to light your candles and incense, and in case of emergency where a fire is desperately needed, we want to advise against lighting a fire. Despite smoke generally being good farther south, here the heat will draw haunts and Mange-creatures straight to you. An amulet enchanted for personal warmth and a Farmlands-woven blanket will help you maintain a certain level of comfort. Despite this, you will crave warm meals and the whistle of the kettle over a crackling fire. These comforts cannot be afforded; you will have to cope. You are in the Hinterlands because you are adventuring, exploring, researching, proving a hypothesis, responding to a personal call...whatever the reason, if you wanted comfort, you would never have left the Belle Flower.

Third, know that your sleep will be little and far between. Your guide will set up watch shifts. Never, never allow your entire party to sleep at the same time, but do ensure that everyone is rested enough that they can think on their paws.

Finally, there is no one place that is better to make camp than another. The woods found along the border provide slightly more overhead protection but are infested with Rats and Mange-creatures. The Muskeg has fewer enemies but is said to have pockets of bogs that suck adventurers into the muck, never to be seen again. The foothills of the Boreal Mountains are freezing, as you must sleep atop tundra; they are also regularly patrolled by Ravens.

Provisions in the Hinterlands

Take provisions that keep for weeks and can be eaten cold. Seed cheese and mushroom jerky are favourite choices. We do not recommend a flask of moonshine, as you should have your wits about you. Some guides have a differing opinion, stating that the modicum of warmth and relaxation provided by a glug of liquor is better than being on edge and restless. Some Home Guard spies are able to harvest mosses from the forests and Muskeg lichen to live off under dire circumstances. Trust only your guide or a Home Guard before you eat anything growing in this area. Much of it is contaminated, even though it may look safe.

Chapter 25: Landmarks of the Hinterlands

WHILE THESE ARE NOT THE SAME KINDS of tourist landmarks as the City or the Farmlands might boast, there are several places that hardy adventurers are drawn to when they journey to the Hinterlands.

The Border Forts

Twelve Border Forts exist along the border between the Scrublands and Hinterlands. The largest and most heavily defended of these is North Fort IV which is build deep into Fort Wood West, a forest of the Border Wood. The Forts are the only area within the forests that are accessible by road—though these are the most heavily enchanted and defended roads in all of Gwelf, and you will pass multiple watchtowers and Home Guard units while walking them. The Guard will likely ask to see your sigils and glyphs, your amulets and talismans, and they may ask for a demonstration of your weapons prowess, but your guide can negotiate these interactions. Regardless, they will strongly encourage you to turn around. If you are so ill prepared as to have no hope of survival, though, you may indeed find yourself with a stern escort back to Dundurn Village.

  The Border Forts are remnants of the pre–Home Guard history, when differing regional militias defended Gwelf from the threat of Ravenkind (if you desire more history, a good resource is Junius Longear's *The Home Guard: A Heroic History*). The forts are ancient structures made of Smoke Pine wood and massive stone, dug into the forests and the land, fortified with spells, runes, gems, and more Particle Magics than exist anywhere else in Gwelf.

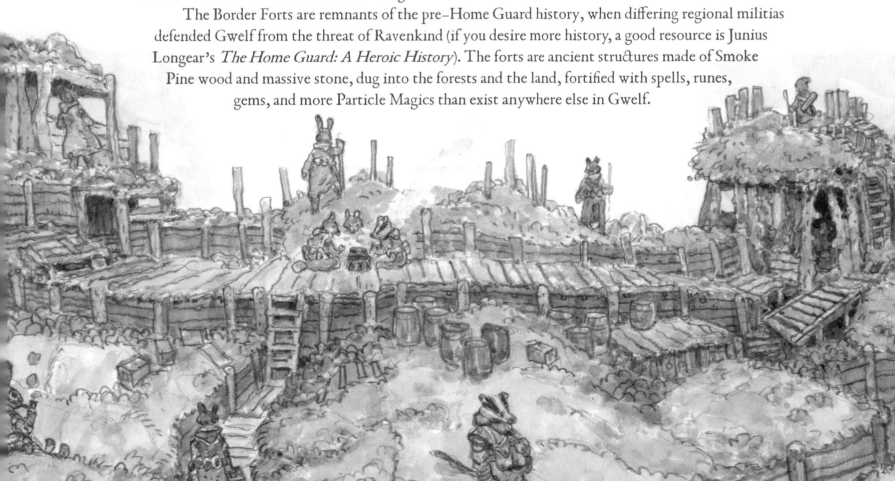

Each fort has a small contingent of Sparrows who oversee operations and coordinate with each other to continue the unified attack on Ravenkind and the protection of Gwelf. It might seem odd, but the flora that grows around the Border Forts rivals the lushest of Farmlands gardens; this is because the Earth Magics practiced by the Sparrows coax life forth, and so much of these magics are focused on and at the forts. In this way the forts can be quite self-sufficient and do not fear siege as much as one might expect.

If you make your way to a Border Fort from the south, you will be welcomed, though perhaps grudgingly. You can trade for fresh provisions and will be given a safe bed to sleep in, but expect to be wished well and sent on your way the next morning. If you arrive at a fort from the north, though, having survived your foray past the border, you will be allowed to stay longer. You will likely be debriefed; while you do not have to answer the questions asked of you by the Sparrows or the Guard, sharing your information is encouraged. The more we know about the enemy, the better.

The Old Witch Tower at Stagtooth

Just to the south of the Border Wood lies the most visited site
of the area, as it is the most reachable by foolhardy tourists.
We cannot stress enough that this is not like the Witch
Market. The Old Witch Tower at Stagtooth was a
meeting place for coven leaders in the long-ago past.
Historical accounts are unclear about the origins of
the haunts here, but the Sparrows and exorcists of the
Home Guard theorize that it was the site of many Steam
Consciousness ventures that went awry. It is assumed
that it was Ravenkind's delving too far into Steam states
that backfired somehow. Here the tortured ghosts of
witches and mages of old have been lingering in agony
for centuries. Their suffering is felt by any who visit
this location, sending new victims into a stupor, or else
chasing the life force right out of them.

The Border Wood

As you venture out of the grassy, lichen-covered Scrublands and
towards the border of the Hinterlands, you will find yourself in
the Border Wood. This wood, which once covered the entire
expanse of the Border Region, is now many smaller forests that
mark the passing between Scrubland and Muskeg. Sources
confirm that this wood was planted by the Sparrows in a time
now lost to memory, the trees nurtured from seedlings harvested
all across Gwelf. It is the strangest mishmash of trees you'll ever
find, including the most northern examples of Smoke Pines, as
well as mighty oaks and ashes, pines from the Old Pine Wood to
the south, and even apple trees (which produce small, hard, sour
apples that'll wake you up in a pinch) and hardy maples, as well
as spruces native to the Hinterlands and Boreals. The trees grow
densely here, and their trunks are so massive that it would take
ten Foxes stretching their paws out as wide as possible to form
a ring around just one.

If you have heard tales of the trees moving, you are not alone. Indeed, the forests of the Border Wood are constantly wracked with a solemn, eerie groaning noise. Some claim this is the sound of roots burrowing faster than any known species of tree, bringing the various arboreal species into diverse configurations. Their goal, it is claimed, is to make it as difficult as possible for Carrion Magics to infiltrate the wood and take hold in Gwelf—or else it is the reverse, and they protect the Hinterlands and Boreals from infiltration from Sparrowkind. Who knows the will of trees?

Many a skeleton can be found in the forests of the Border Wood, belonging to those unlucky adventurers who did not equip themselves properly or hire a guide. Getting lost in the woods, even getting squeezed and trapped between the trunks of two moving trees, is commonplace here. Running into ancient ghosts with the power to drain the warmth and the life from you has been reported as well. And of course, being caught and kidnapped by the Ravenkind hiding in the woods is the worst fate of all.

There are no maps of the Border Wood. There are no written foraging guides. The wood exists as a barrier, nurtured and protected by its own will to thrive. It acts as a sort of wild first line of defence between Sparrowkind and Ravenkind, or perhaps vice versa.

The Muskeg

North of the Border Wood and its forests lies an area known only as the Muskeg. This area is in constant flux as it is a wetland. Some describe it as a tropical swamp, others a temperate marshland, others a rocky tundra. All agree it has a strong peaty odour. Hunks of wood, dying cattails, dead and stunted trees, and spongy moss have all been reported. Many who have made it back from the Muskeg say it is in a constant fog, and that the fog is often strangely coloured. Many say they can hear voices, laughter, and song within the fog.

    It is from the Muskeg that strange lumbering creatures have been spotted. We have provided a sketch here that Wilburton made from a description given by a Home Guard patrol having just returned to the Border Fort. We do not know these creatures, but they act like agents of Ravenkind, so beware.

Ragtooth Trolls

Beyond the Boreals

The Ravens fled to the Boreal Mountains to practice their own magics in their own way. Their magics, suffused in death and corruption as they are, require living victims upon which to experiment. That, along with a desire for revenge for the betrayal they still keenly feel, drives the Ravens to invade and attack Gwelf and disrupt Sparrowkind society. We hope to have provided you with some inkling of the danger that lies beyond the border—the Hinterlands, containing Muskeg, Boreal Mountains, and beyond: in short, the places from which very few creatures return.

CITY OF GWELF

GWELF COUNCIL for TOURISM and TRADE

Afterword

When the Council came to me to illustrate this guide, I leapt at the chance. Having only been in Gwelf a short time and eager for an assignment, this seemed like the perfect opportunity to acquaint myself with my newly adopted home. There were many times that I would regret my choice to complete this project. The ghosts of the Scrublands were, in particular, quite shocking and off-putting, and I often found myself wishing that I'd stayed at home, safe by the fire with a mug of hot tea. But I am back now, safe and sound, and the job is done—though there is always more to do and see in Gwelf. I chose to put myself in many of these drawings to prove I was there. I'm glad I went and I regret nothing, despite the many harrowing moments and lingering haunting memories. I was chosen because I was new to Gwelf, searching for an artist contract, and willing to adventure. It was hoped that my fresh perspective would bring an immediacy and urgency to the work. I believe it has. The reportage is true and of the moment.

We are preparing for a second book now in order to complete some sections of Gwelf that I have not yet had the chance to visit, and to once again trek past my own comforts into the Hinterlands and beyond, into the Boreals. I will embark with a deep reconnaissance team of adventurers and ex–Home Guards. I can say no more about it here, as there is no telling if a Rat or Raven spy might get hold of this text. The thought of this new adventure brings with it the same trepidation and dread I felt many times during the making of this first guide, and yet the same excitement and yearning for adventure is growing within me. I can't resist the call to action. Can you?

Wilburton Fox
September 20, Belle Flower Inn, Gwelf

THE GWELF SKETCHBOOK

Binoculars

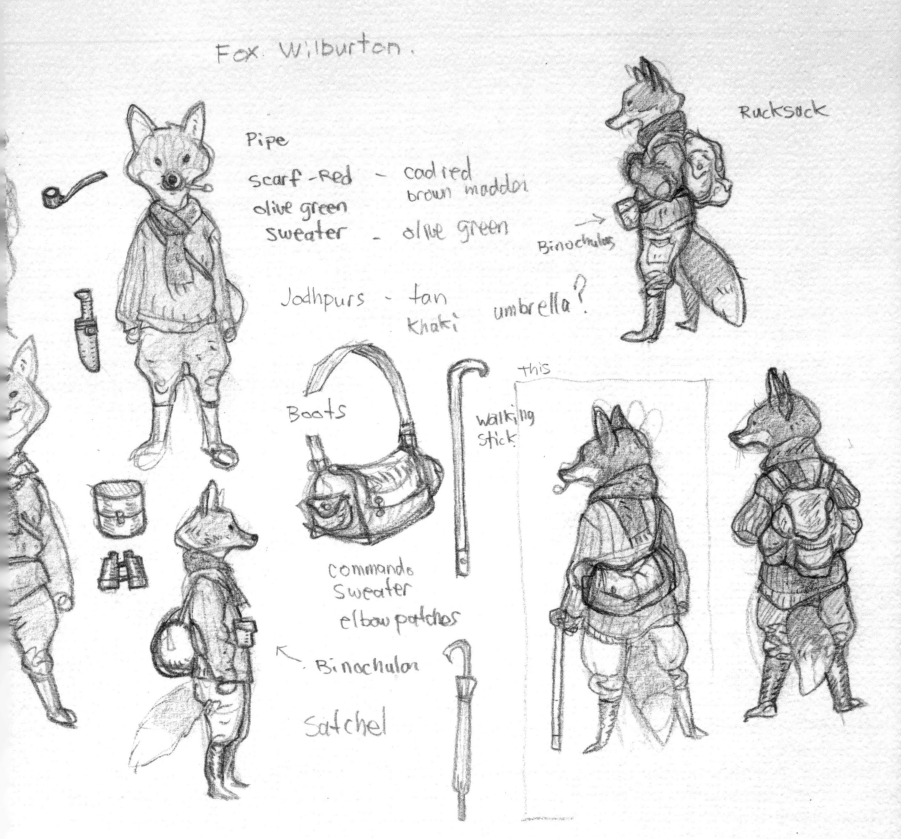

Fox Wilburton.

Pipe

scarf - Red   — cadred
olive green   brown madder
sweater   - olive green

Jodhpurs - tan
             khaki   umbrella?

Rucksack

→ Binoculars

Boots

commando
sweater
elbow patches

walking
stick

this

← Binoculars

Satchel

Sparrow.

- Sparrows
Magic.   - mysterious,

Boreal Zombie Hunter

Patrol

Ragtooth.

Ragtooth attack

About the Author

LARRY MacDOUGALL entered the commercial art world approximately thirty years ago and has been very busy ever since. He began working for gaming publishers, contributing work to many projects in the Dungeons and Dragons vein. Larry was content with this work for many years but gradually the games began to take on a violent and darker tone. This is when he decided to leave the gaming world and cross over to children's publishing where he illustrated many books for publishers both in Canada and abroad. For the last fifteen years Larry has been working as an animation designer, book illustrator, environment and character designer for games, and fine artist making personal art for private clients. He has also been dreaming up the world of Gwelf.

Now he is embarking on that adventure and inviting you to come along.

www.eyeofnewtpress.com